He stood half-naked on her balcony....

The wind-driven rain followed Tripp as he entered her room. Lightning blazed and for a moment, Abby could see him clearly. Wearing only a pair of dark cutoffs soaked by the rain, he looked hard, desperate…dangerous. If he'd been a stranger, she would have been terrified.

But he wasn't a stranger. Not anymore. And she wanted to bring him inside. To touch him. To have him touch her. As if he read the welcome in her eyes, he shoved the door shut, closing out the storm behind him.

A second later, his hands were on her, pulling her to him. The moisture on his chest soaked through her gown as his mouth closed over hers. As one searing kiss melded into another, heat slithered through her, making her breasts ache and her knees weak. She heard a low, yearning whimper and realized it had come from her. Her body pleading for what Tripp could give her, with his mouth, his hands, his body.

Tripp recognized the sound of surrender. He could feel it on her warm skin, taste it in her soft, hot mouth. He knew he shouldn't be here. The tequila he'd had earlier had made him reckless. But now, after touching her, he couldn't leave.

Not until he'd been inside her and felt her explode around him....

SUPER ROMANCE

"As a kid who grew up in South Florida, I spent many summers visiting the Keys," says talented author **Lyn Ellis**. "And what better setting could I use for my first Temptation Blaze than Florida—a place known for its sultry ocean-breeze days and even hotter tropical nights. Actually," she admits, "I take a lot of teasing from the rest of my family. Although I love the sun, surf and sand, I'm definitely a landlubber at heart. When the rest of the family goes out scuba diving, I prefer to be left *in* the boat!"

Books by Lyn Ellis

HARLEQUIN TEMPTATION
488—DEAR JOHN
532—IN PRAISE OF YOUNGER MEN
575—MICHAEL'S ANGEL
615—CHRISTMAS KNIGHT
618—NEW YEAR'S KNIGHT

Lyn Ellis
NIGHT HEAT

Harlequin Books

TORONTO • NEW YORK • LONDON
AMSTERDAM • PARIS • SYDNEY • HAMBURG
STOCKHOLM • ATHENS • TOKYO • MILAN
MADRID • WARSAW • BUDAPEST • AUCKLAND

ISBN 0-373-25766-X

NIGHT HEAT

Copyright © 1998 by Gin Ellis.

This edition published by arrangement with Harlequin Books S.A.

® and TM are trademarks of the publisher. Trademarks indicated with
® are registered in the United States Patent and Trademark Office, the
Canadian Trade Marks Office and in other countries.

Printed in U.S.A.

_____Prologue_____

HE KNEW she'd be there.

It was his job to look out for her. To watch the ocean, the house, the boats. Her.

Tripp Anderson moved out of the sunlight and into the shade of a gumbo-limbo as Abby Duncan dropped her towel and glasses on a lawn chair. He leaned a bare shoulder against the dark smooth bark as she stepped up to the edge of the pool, straightened, then made a perfect arcing dive into the still water. With a splash she disappeared.

A trickle of sweat rolled down Tripp's spine. The morning sun was already a hot glare on the ocean and the water in the pool. And he'd just run four miles.

He knew he should turn around and run four more, until Abby was out of the pool, out of his sight, out of his thoughts. But he didn't move as she broke the surface and began her ritual laps. He waited.

The scowling face of Carlos Cezare, the attorney who'd hired him, flashed through his mind. Carlos was very big on honor. Tripp knew it would be difficult to justify, as part of his job description, watching Abby swim. Being a bodyguard didn't mean he needed to see quite so much of Abby's body. But hell, Carlos was an old married man. He probably thought all women should swim fully clothed—to prevent men from watching, from fantasizing just as Tripp was doing.

Carlos didn't have to worry. Tripp would never touch Abby, and he'd never tell her what Carlos had hired him to do. He'd given his word. His job consisted of keeping her safe from men like her ex-fiancé who'd wanted her money, or from—in Carlos's words—unsuitable men who merely wanted her. Unfortunately, Tripp fit into the latter category. And that meant he had to protect her from himself as well. He'd been caught in the I've-got-to-have-you trap before, by his ex-partner's wife. He'd turned her down, but it had cost him: his business, his boat, his dream of sailing around the world. Now, with Abby, he recognized the same symptoms in himself, and he knew he had to avoid the complications by avoiding her.

But the sight of her sleek, wet body in the demure tank suit had drawn him every morning. And, as long as she never knew, he could indulge himself.

And he did. When Abby hiked herself to a sitting position at the edge of the pool, Tripp watched the water sluice down her skin. He stood there sweating while she used the fluffy towel to scrub the drops from her legs and arms, then wrapped the cloth around her. He watched her walk down the path, back to the main house of the resort before he made his way to the dock, kicked off his running shoes and dove into the ocean.

He couldn't use the pool, not right after she'd left it. Not when the thought of being in that water with her was pumping through his blood. That would be getting too close. And he knew about getting too close. His job was to look out for her and to keep his hands to himself.

He could do that. No sweat.

1

THE LONG, ELEGANT DONZI powerboat skimmed over
the waves like a seabird flying fast and low. Abby Duncan turned her face into the wind, enjoying the salty
spray, the bright afternoon sun and the sheer power of
the engines.

She glanced sideways toward the impassive man
driving the boat she'd inherited along with several
acres of paradise called Leah's Cay. There was something fascinating about watching a man handle a car, or
a boat. Something about control and concentration, and
confidence. Tripp knew more about boats than most
Conchs. He stood at ease, perfectly balanced with his
feet braced apart. He was wearing cutoffs, and Abby
couldn't help but admire the muscles delineated in his
thighs and calves—the legs of a runner.

She'd seen him run early in the mornings, but rarely
had the opportunity to view him up close since he
seemed determined to stay away from the main house.
A loner. He'd come with her inheritance—hired and
paid by her lawyer. Because of that, and because of the
way he handled the boat, Abby trusted him implicitly...at least on the water.

The engines changed pitch as they made a wide turn

toward the channel markers. When they reached the first set, Tripp throttled back, and the boat rose on its own wake as it slowed. Abby shaded her eyes with her hand and looked toward their destination, the Pelican Bar and Marina on Long Key.

"I'll drop you off dockside, then go around to gas up," Tripp said as the shadow of the Long Key bridge flicked over them. "I've got to pick up the extra air tanks I had filled."

"Okay. Anything you want me to tell Jimmy?"

Tripp slowed the boat even more as they turned into the "no wake" zone of the marina. "Yeah, tell him to make sure there's plenty of bait on board and a couple of sharp knives." The corners of his eyes crinkled behind his mirrored sunglasses, but he didn't actually smile. "Since he can't act as mate, he can prop his cast up on a cooler and cut bait."

Abby rolled her eyes. Tripp had been the one who'd mentioned to her that Jimmy Rittner had wrecked his leg on a motorcycle and couldn't captain his charter boat. Abby had a group of sport fisherman checking into the resort for the week and she needed something to take them out on. Every day that Jimmy's boat sat at the dock, he lost money. So, according to Tripp, the perfect solution seemed to be for Abby to rent the boat and for Tripp to captain the charter.

Unlike her former fiancé, Tripp rarely made suggestions about the resort unless it was along the lines of boat maintenance. Even though he seemed content to stay in his own domain and out of her business, she had the feeling there was more to him than his affinity for watercraft. This time he'd spoken up for Jimmy, so naturally she assumed he was a friend of Tripp's, but she couldn't be sure. As odd as it seemed, even to her, she had no idea what Tripp did when he left Leah's Cay.

One of the boys who worked at the marina caught the bow rope before the boat touched the bumpers at the dock. "Hey, how you guys doin'?" he asked as he braced one sneakered foot against the bow and extended a hand to Abby. "Nice ride you got there."

"Thanks," Abby answered. In many ways she felt like the boat belonged more to Tripp than to her. The adjustment from making ends meet to owning all the ends had taken longer than she'd expected. She didn't know how to "live large." Her only experience had been through her best friend, Leah, and Leah's father. And now they were gone, leaving her everything, and she had to figure it out alone.

Inheriting money hadn't changed Abby—it had only changed her perceived value in the eyes of others. Before learning that lesson, she'd nearly married a man intent on relieving her of her inheritance any way he could. She'd found out, nearly too late, that Larry wanted to liquidate everything and move to Bermuda to escape the IRS.

What doesn't kill you, makes you stronger...and more cautious. Abby was most definitely alive and rich, and...alone. She wished for the thousandth time that she'd wake up from this dream and see Leah walk in the front door of the home she'd loved. Or that Abby could ask Leah's father for advice on how to protect the money and property he'd worked so hard to acquire.

But she'd had to do the best she could, alone.

Her own beginnings in Cullowee, North Carolina, had been much more humble. She'd gotten a scholarship to pursue her dream of a marketing career at an Ivy League school, and two things had happened during her four-year pursuit. Her father had died and she'd met Leah Axillar.

Now, because her mother preferred the North Carolina mountains to paradise in the Florida Keys, Abby was on her own.

Rather than living in the mansion by herself, Abby had turned it into an exclusive retreat. She found she had more talent at being the boss of a resort than in managing the personal ramifications of the Axillar fortune she'd inherited. Thank heavens she had "Grumpy" Cezare, the Axillar family lawyer, to handle the holdings and investments, even if he was a nosy old curmudgeon. She'd discovered the hard way, that dictatorial or not, Carlos was the only person she could trust. The only person who wanted what was best for "her." She'd even talked him into cooperating with her lie. As far as anyone else knew, she only managed the four-star resort at Leah's Cay—and she was good at it.

Abby picked up her oversize bag and allowed the boy to help her onto the dock. Then she turned to Tripp and waved. "Shouldn't take long."

The businesswoman in her noticed that most of the boat slips were empty—which meant the crews were out working. Jimmy's boat, the *Miss Behavin'*, looked battened down and deserted. She made her way to that end of the dock.

In the shade of an awning connected to a small office, two men loudly debated some point about the Marlins in particular and baseball in general. A bright slice of afternoon light illuminated the cast on the infamous Captain Jimmy "Billfish" Rittner's leg, propped on an overturned bucket. Another shorter, heavier man dressed in cutoffs and a flowered, Hawaiian-style shirt leaned against the building next to him.

As she approached, the conversation Jimmy had been involved in ended abruptly. His gaze met hers before drifting downward briefly, from her head, to bare legs, to her sandals and pink polished toenails.

He frowned.

She extended her hand. "Hi, Jimmy. I'm Abby Duncan—"

"Yeah, I know. From Leah's Cay." He used one large hand to engulf hers. Jimmy's expression looked much more serious than the occasion. "Tripp told me about you," he said.

"He did?" The thought of Tripp describing her came as a surprise. He seemed to be totally oblivious to her most of the time. It was on the tip of her tongue to ask *how* he'd described her, but she changed her mind. Probably better not to know.

"Sorry—" Jimmy raised a hand to indicate his leg "—I can't get up." He then reached sideways and yanked another lawn chair closer, to face him. "Have a seat."

She sat, then pulled out the checkbook she'd brought with her. "I came by to give you a check."

The man who'd been leaning against the wall straightened and said, "You can just make that check out to me." Jimmy gave him an unfriendly look and seemed about to tell him to back off, when the guy spoke again. "He owes me."

Abby had no intention of getting acquainted with this man or his business with Jimmy Rittner. Ignoring the man's comment, she finished filling in the check, tore it from the book and held it out to Jimmy.

The heavyset guy smiled and snatched the check from her hand. Before Abby could do more than be shocked at his rudeness, a voice came from behind her. "Give it back."

It seemed like the ocean, the cars on the road nearby, even the seagulls, went silent at those words. Jimmy Rittner seemed transfixed, staring over her shoulder, so Abby turned.

Tripp. She'd recognized his voice, sort of, though she'd never heard that deadly tone before.

He slowly removed his sunglasses but kept his gaze on the man who'd snatched her check. Startled by the cold, vivid blue of his eyes, Abby realized she didn't really know this man. He'd worked for her for more than six months, and she'd had no idea how threatening he could be. And she was supremely grateful that in the few instances he'd looked at her directly, he hadn't been angry at the time.

"I said...give the lady her check."

Unable to derail whatever was about to happen, Abby shifted her gaze to the man holding the disputed check and held her breath as he spent a long thirty seconds sizing Tripp up. He didn't seem to like what he saw.

His hand jerked once, and he smiled nervously. "Hey, man—" he gingerly offered the check to Abby "—don't get your B.V.D.s in a wad. I'm not poaching. This is none of your business. It's between Jimmy and me."

"She's my business," Tripp said in that same even tone. "You mess with her, you mess with me."

"That's cool. I'm not lookin' for trouble." With another smile that didn't look friendly and a wave that resembled a salute, he turned and sauntered back to his position against the wall.

Abby stood and extended the check to Jimmy. She went on as if the man had never interfered. "You'll pick up Tripp and the guests at 6:00 a.m. on Saturday?"

Jimmy cleared his throat. "Yeah, sure. Listen, I'm sorry about that." Then he faced Tripp. "I guess I owe you an explanation."

Tripp nodded. "Later," he said, and replaced his sunglasses. Case closed. He raised one hand toward the Donzi, now tied at the dock. "Ready to go?" he asked Abby.

A rhetorical question at best. She *was* ready to go.

Tripp's voice still sounded tight, and after seeing his intimidating side firsthand, the promise of a free vacation with Mel Gibson couldn't have kept her on this dock another moment.

As usual, Tripp didn't touch her, not even to help her into the boat. He let the dock boy handle it. Soon they were flying over the open water again, without conversation.

Safely on her way home, Abby could see the humor in the confrontation. Maybe because he'd surprised her, she couldn't resist a jab at the taciturn man she'd seen mutate from laid-back boat captain to defender of her honor.

She smiled as she propped an arm on the console and faced Tripp. "'You mess with her, you mess with me,'" she said, making a bad attempt to imitate his tough-guy tone. "What's up with that?" she asked unable to hold back a laugh. "I never knew you cared."

For several heartbeats he kept driving the boat, as if the wind had blown away her words. Then he turned and looked at her briefly. Abby experienced the unnerving effect of seeing her own face reflected in his mirrored glasses. Rather than joining in on the joke, he seemed even less talkative than usual, or maybe still angry.

"It's my responsibility," he said before turning his attention back to the water in front of them. "If I'd known Jimmy was in some kind of trouble, I never would have set this up."

"Is he in trouble?"

Tripp shrugged. "He probably bet on the wrong horse or lost a fishing tournament. Whatever it is, there's no need for you or me to get involved. You paid good money to rent his boat. It's up to him what he does with it."

They approached Leah's Cay from the oceanside. The island, about three hundred yards off Long Key, was connected to dry land by a single-laned, gravel road walled by mangrove trees. But the front of the estate and the house faced the ocean so that from the main entrance stretched only green lawn, tropical blue water and sky.

Paradise.

Palm trees stood like sentries to the left and right of the concrete dock that was large enough to accommodate several boats, including the fifty-two-foot Bene-teau sailboat and the Donzi Tripp was guiding home.

Abby took the bow rope and jumped to the dock to hold the boat close as Tripp shut down the engines. He did the same with the stern rope, and after a few swift movements to tie his end, he stepped toward her and took the rope from her hand. He squatted down to tie it.

"I guess I should thank you," she said as she watched his tan fingers work the rope over the davit.

He paused and looked up at her, and she found herself staring at his mouth since she couldn't see his eyes. His lips were firmly drawn into a straight line and his jaw looked tight. Abby wondered whether he ever smiled. He'd certainly never smiled at her.

With a mental shake, she breezed by the implication

that he wasn't interested in being friends with her. What difference did that make? Grumpy had sent him to take care of the boats and to tell the lawn crews what to do. Tripp was just an employee. He didn't even live in the main house. He had his own small guest house among the palm trees closer to the water.

But he hadn't been just an employee today. He'd surprised her at the marina by defending her. Now her curiosity had been aroused, and she wanted to know if there were any other surprises in store.

"No problem," he said. "Like I said, if chartering Jimmy's boat gets too complicated, we'll find another. There are a lot of other boats looking for work." He stood up and braced his hands on his hips. "Anything else?"

Feeling dismissed instead of having done the dismissing, Abby shrugged, then pulled her bag higher on her shoulder. She'd save her questions...for a while. "No. See ya later," she said, and turned toward the house.

Tripp watched Abby walk away and felt like kicking himself. Wait until he got his hands on Jimmy Rittner. He'd be lucky if Tripp didn't break his other leg for him.

It was Tripp's job to keep an eye on things around Leah's Cay, and whether she knew it or not, that included the boss lady. Then today, his little charitable enterprise to help Jimmy had almost caused more trouble than it was worth.

Damn. After losing everything in the name of friendship, he should have known better. To test the knot one more time, he prodded the rope holding the Donzi, then brushed his hands together. He was still furious—at Jimmy, and at that flower-shirted creep who seemed to enjoy intimidating women. When Tripp had seen him jerk the check from Abby's hand, he'd wanted to drag the guy behind the building for a few serious lessons in manners. Lessons that included one or two broken bones. That feeling worried him. He'd built his reputation on being logical, cool, immune to overreaction. And his reputation was about all he had left.

And now Abby had started asking questions.

He didn't want her to thank him or tease him, or ask him if he cared. The best thing would be not to talk at all. The vision of her, smooth and wet, coming out of the pool ambushed him. He deliberately pushed that memory out of his thoughts. Wanting her was just a physical thing. He had to stick to business, strictly business. But it had gone beyond business today. Witnessing any man trying to push Abby around had set Tripp off.

Worse than that, Abby had noticed.

The last time a business associate—his partner's wife—had noticed him, all hell had broken loose. It couldn't happen again, he wouldn't allow it. He had too much riding on this job, on his deal with Carlos Cezare. All Tripp had to do was sit tight, trade six months of his life watching Abby, and Carlos would use his powerful Miami old-money connections to get Tripp's boat back.

He gazed out toward the ocean and the sky. *Get over it*, he ordered himself under his breath. *It was no big deal, just the usual macho intimidation dance. By this time tomorrow it'll be ancient history.* Then he glanced back over his shoulder in time to see Abby turn and look at him briefly before opening the door to the main house. "No big deal," he said out loud, as if that would make everything fine again.

2

"WHAT DO YOU KNOW about Tripp?" Abby asked Louisa, the official cook of Leah's Cay, as they chopped vegetables for dinner. Louisa's daughter, Julia, hurried through the room carrying an armload of clean towels.

"Not much," Louisa answered, preoccupied. "He seems nice enough." She stopped to stir the tomato base bubbling on the stove. "He helped my son fix his car once when it broke down on the way to pick me up. He knows a lot about cars."

Abby almost laughed. Boats and cars—as far as she knew, Tripp had no other life. Did he read books? Have a girlfriend?

Louisa suddenly stopped and looked at Abby. "Why? Is something wrong?"

Abby did laugh then. Just as it had merely taken Abby one small incident to see Tripp in a different light, it had taken one innocent question to start Louisa worrying. "No. Nothing, really. I just realized that I don't know much about him, that's all."

"You should ask Mr. Cezare," Louisa suggested.

"Yeah, I guess I should," Abby agreed. She knew Grumpy would have investigated Tripp before he'd hired him. But somehow that course seemed underhanded. And she had the feeling Tripp wouldn't appreciate it. If she wanted to know about him, she ought to simply ask him. Yet, the memory of how he'd looked at the marina when he'd been angry made asking him questions seem foolhardy. Abby decided to let it go for the time being.

"Right now, though, we've got other fish to fry, literally and figuratively. We have a busy week coming up. Dolores and her girls will be back from their cruise on Sunday. Our honeymooners will be in tomorrow night. I want them to have special attention." Abby wiped her hands on a towel and looked at the clock. "And, the men from Philadelphia will be in anytime."

"Well, we're as ready as we'll ever be." Louisa smiled. "Do you suppose any of these Philadelphia men are single?"

Abby met Louisa's amused gaze with a frown. "I certainly hope not—they're lawyers. One lawyer in my life, Grumpy, is all I can stand and keep my sanity. Besides—" she wagged one threatening finger at Louisa "—they're here to fish. And that's my plan for them. They want fishing? They'll get fishing. All the bait and boats they can stand."

LAWYERS, Tripp thought in disgust. He popped open the top of his second beer and took a swig before bending to check his fishing pole. The tension on the line remained constant—not even a nibble.

He'd spent over an hour with the new 'guests' after

they'd had dinner. Showing them the boats, stowing their gear and talking tides.

He'd been polite, even though he already had a built-in attitude about lawyers. After the cost and ineffective shuffling of his own lawyers who couldn't manage to save his business, he didn't care if he ever met another one. The fact that Carlos Cezare, the granddaddy of all lawyers in Tripp's estimation, was willing to take his case, with a few unusual stipulations, didn't change Tripp's basic attitude problem. He would do anything it took to get his boat back. But putting up with three legal eagles from some fat-cat firm in Philadelphia would be a demanding test of his patience.

And then Abby had shown up.

Tripp gazed at the quarter moon hanging in the clear sky and sighed. It was late, close to midnight he figured, and the tide was going out. He wedged the pole between the rocks again. Soon the mosquitoes would find him and he'd have more bites on his skin than on his fishing line.

But he wasn't sleepy. He'd been edgy most of the evening. Truth be told, he'd been out of sorts since the incident at the marina with Jimmy and his bully buddy. But now he had a new problem.

One of the lawyers couldn't seem to keep his eyes off Abby. From the moment she'd strolled down to the dock, the man had smiled and flirted with her.

Tripp had almost forgotten to be polite. He rubbed a hand down his face and took another sip of his beer.

He'd have to keep an eye on that—the lawyer, and his own reaction to the man's interest in Abby.

The first stinging mosquito bite brought him back to the matter at hand. The wind had died completely, and the fish seemed to be ignoring his bait. Several miles eastward over the Atlantic, silent streaks of heat lightning illuminated the clouds.

Tripp poured the last of his beer out and began reeling in his line. He wished it would go ahead and rain, to end the tense stillness. He needed to get some sleep. Maybe he should run a few miles to short-circuit his edginess. Swim some laps. He folded up his lawn chair, snapped his tackle box closed and headed back toward the dock by a narrow trail through the mangroves.

ABBY STEPPED OUT of the side door and drew in a deep breath. She saw lightning in the distance. The air had gone still, like it did sometimes before a storm, and the ever-rustling palm trees drooped in silence. Each small noise seemed to carry, and her own footsteps crunching on the gravel sounded too loud in her ears. She stepped onto the grass and moved toward the dock, toward the ocean.

She'd gotten the fishermen settled and promised them a wake-up call. It had been a long day of traveling for them and a full day of work for her. She'd spent the better part of the morning helping Julia transform one of the larger suites in the mansion into a fantasy boudoir fit to grace any ad in *Bride's* magazine. From peach satin sheets, extra pillows and scented candles to oversize towels and bubble bath, they had tried to anticipate any luxury the honeymooners might appreciate.

So why wasn't she settled in and sleeping? She'd gotten undressed, taken a shower and stretched out on her bed with a book. But she'd ended up staring out the window into the night, remembering the plans she'd made for her own wedding, her own honeymoon. Finally, too restless to sleep, she'd pulled on a pair of shorts and a T-shirt and decided to walk.

It wasn't just the honeymooners. Rick, one of the guests, reminded her of Larry—her ex-fiancé and all-around fortune hunter type of guy. The image of Larry's practiced smile rose in her mind and close behind that she remembered the day his smile had disappeared, the day she'd opened a file in her lawyer's office and found out how completely he'd fooled her.

She didn't miss being lied to, even if it was done subtly and with her own well-being in mind. She missed the idea of being a couple. Of getting married and having a "normal" life.

She paused in her stroll and glanced back toward the graceful mansion behind her. Soft light glowed through the glass block panels framing the front door. An extraordinary house built with taste and care, filled with every luxury money could buy. Several steps beyond normal.

Her friend Leah's life, like her home, hadn't been normal, either. All through college she'd been the poor little rich girl, shadowed by bodyguards, kept separate by the power of her father's name. Abby had loved her humor, her intelligence, her fierce loyalty to a friend who had next to nothing. But she'd seen Leah's loneliness. Abby should have known better than to think her own life could be ordinary after inheriting everything most people dreamed of having—money, paradise, total freedom. But she'd thought she could keep the money separate, that her personal life still belonged to her. She'd been a fool.

So, after learning the lesson with Larry, the hard way, she'd taken steps to protect herself by concocting her own lie. She'd lie to everyone first, before they had the chance to fool her again. Then she'd teach herself to like being alone.

Now, here she was faced with another good-looking lawyer with a practiced smile. Rick. Did he have a file on her? Did he know that she wasn't really the manager of Leah's Cay, but the owner? Did he think he could charm his way into her life, into her money? Leah's money? The thought of that type of calculation gave her a chill inside. She'd never get used to being a juicy target, but she wouldn't be fooled again. By anyone.

Abby stepped onto the concrete dock and faced the water, a view that usually calmed her. Yet tonight she felt restless. Even the ever-changing ocean seemed still. The water level had dropped, as if someone had pulled a huge plug out there somewhere. Small, whispering waves lapped along the boats.

Abby lifted the limp weight of her hair off her neck and sighed. Where was the breeze? The humidity felt thick enough to swim through—like the water in the pool.

The sound of the door to the boathouse closing startled her. She squinted through the darkness, and her heart lurched in her chest before she recognized Tripp. She should have known it was him. But the darkness and the late hour made any noise suspect. As he walked in the opposite direction without acknowledging her, she realized she'd know his back anywhere, because he always seemed to be walking away from her. Doing his job, busy, on his way...somewhere else.

Being his boss didn't give her the right to ask him what he did with his own time. Still, she wondered what he'd been doing so late. Expecting him to follow the walkway to his guest house, it surprised her when he stopped at the place where he should have turned right. After a slight hesitation, he continued on.

Where was he going now?

Before Abby made a conscious decision, she started down the walk behind him. She didn't slow down until she'd almost reached the pool. What did she think she was doing? If he caught her, Tripp would assume she was checking up on him...or spying.

She stopped. There were no voices.... The entire planet seemed hushed. Tripp's steady footsteps had stopped. Unable to resist, Abby stepped off the walk and into the trees.

Through the branches, she saw him just as he whipped his shirt over his head, his back to her, as always. Not by choice this time, but by fate. The dim light from the moon and a distant security light at the front of the house illuminated the area enough for her to see the play of muscle in his shoulders and the lean line of his waist.

Abby braced herself against a tree to keep from moving and making any sound. Obviously he intended to swim in the pool, alone, under the moon, and he probably wouldn't appreciate an audience. But she couldn't take her eyes off him.

Then he unfastened his cutoffs and dropped them. Startled by the sight of his nude backside, Abby caught her breath. She knew her face must be scarlet, because she felt like a five-year-old seeing a naked boy for the first time. Wicked. The adult in her said she shouldn't look, she should walk away before someone caught her.

But, God, he was beautiful...and the woman in her acknowledged that he was definitely a man. Why hadn't she thought about him in that way? Well, of course because she hadn't seen him naked but... Before she could decide whether it would be a good thing or a bad thing for him to turn and face her, he dove into the pool.

With long sure strokes he set out for the opposite end. Abby could only see ripples in the water and his dark head along with the occasional pale flash of his naked backside. She felt as though a stranger had invaded her night—swimming naked in her pool. The pool she visited every morning. The pool that would never look the same to her even in broad daylight.

Now she knew why she'd been so restless, what she

really missed about being a couple. She missed that elemental male-female pull. She missed sex. Why had she thought she could stay busy with the resort, give up men in principle because she'd been fooled? Her body hadn't forgotten. And now she'd been forcibly, yet innocently reminded. By an unlikely candidate in the form of Tripp—the boatman.

Tripp swam back to her end of the pool and stopped. She saw him rake his wet hair back with one hand and draw in a deep breath. When he braced both hands on the side of the pool, she realized he was about to get out. If she didn't want to know every single detail about his body, from all sides, she needed to leave—fast. How in the world would she ever be able to look him in the eye again?

She tried to be quiet as she stepped toward the walkway, but in the silence of the night her movement through the undergrowth sounded like an elephant stampede. She stopped and glanced back. It seemed even Tripp had noticed something. He'd paused and was staring at the trees. He couldn't possibly see her. Could he? But what if he decided to check out the noise? Losing the self-appointed nerve that had prompted her to follow him in the first place, she took off at a trot back toward the house. He'd have to run across the estate naked to catch her.

TRIPP CAUGHT a glimpse of her as she cut across the lawn. Standing on the walk with his clothes in his hand, he couldn't chase her. And what would he say if he could? She'd seen him in the pool. Her pool. Naked.

He used his T-shirt to dry off and wondered about the consequences. Would she decide he was some kind of nudist weirdo and fire him? He could just imagine the blistering phone call he'd get from Carlos. Then he'd never see his boat again.

He'd turned back to retrieve his shoes when the cosmic humor of it struck him. She'd been watching *him*. The idea of her eyes on him caused an instant reaction in his body. Hot and hard. The male in him hoped she'd gotten an eyeful, payback for the torture he'd gone through watching her. She must have seen more than she'd expected if her hasty retreat meant anything. How long had she been there?

Then he remembered his job. He was supposed to be watching out for her. What in the hell had she been doing wandering around outside alone after midnight? Or, had she been looking for someone else and accidentally found him?

Fully dressed again, Tripp strolled along the edge of the trees until he could look up at Abby's window. He watched as the light in her room came on briefly, then went out. He wondered if the sheets on her bed smelled like the ocean, like her. And whether she was lying in the dark thinking about what she'd seen at the pool. Then he wondered if she knew how lucky they both were, that she was inside and safe, from everything…especially him.

3

ABBY OPENED HER EYES at 4:00 a.m.

She wasn't supposed to wake the guests for their fishing trip until four-thirty, but she hadn't slept well. Dreams. The ocean. She'd dreamed she'd been swimming in the ocean. Floating, calm and warm, everything peaceful. Then the tranquil water had churned into rough waves and strong hands were reaching for her. She'd woken up hot, grasping thin air, yearning for the touch of those hands.

She shrugged off the twisted sheets, sat up and glanced out the window. After a night of stillness, the breeze had returned. The palm trees near Abby's balcony rustled in the predawn darkness and the sound calmed her. She was on dry land, in control of her own life. She didn't need those hands to save her, to hold her.

The image of Tripp's naked back materialized in her thoughts, and she closed her eyes to savor it. Lean, yet muscular—a swimmer's shoulders. Even the memory had the power to warm her, from the inside out. She'd wanted to know more about him, but she'd seen more than she'd expected, right down to his naked backside. And without his permission. How in the world could she face him after spying on him? After nearly seeing everything...

She covered her face and shook her head. Thank goodness he hadn't caught her. How embarrassing. She had no excuses, no way to explain her sudden fascination with one of her employees, a man she'd practically ignored for months. She pushed up from the bed, walked to the doors leading to the balcony and opened them. The darkness around the grounds was complete. She couldn't even blame her craziness on the full moon.

Just remember, curiosity killed the cat, she reminded herself. *Or was that, let sleeping dogs lie? Whatever.* She shut the doors and switched on the light. No more curiosity concerning Tripp. She'd seen enough. She didn't want to know what else he did in her pool at midnight.

TRIPP WAS BENDING over an open cooler when Abby stepped into the mansion's spacious kitchen an hour later. The sight of his backside, covered this time, sent Abby's heart into triple time. *Act normal. He doesn't know you were watching him,* her logic declared, even as she stumbled on the last step leading down into the room.

The noise increased as Tripp dumped ice and packed drinks into the cooler to take on the boat. Keeping her back to him, she busied herself making coffee. After measuring water and scoops of imported grounds, Abby was forced to turn. She watched as Tripp bent again and picked up the heavy cooler. He stopped abruptly when he saw her.

He wasn't wearing the ever-present sunglasses,

Abby realized. And to her chagrin, for once, he looked directly at her. In the moment of silence that followed, Abby could feel warmth pooling in her cheeks. *Say something, you idiot!* her mind screamed. But her voice had failed her the moment she'd looked into his eyes. She felt as naked as he'd been the night before.

He knew she'd been watching him. She didn't know how he knew, but he knew.

"Good morning," he said, and waited. He was dressed in a T-shirt that had been customized by the sleeves having been cut away from shoulder to waist, and the muscles in his upper arms bulged from the weight of the cooler.

Abby's throat went dry. *Good morning? What was that supposed to mean?* she wondered in panic. He'd never gone out of his way to wish her a good anything. "Good morning," she finally managed to squeeze out, then pasted a brief, hopefully ordinary smile on her face. Before he could say anything else, Julia entered the kitchen and started setting out the muffins, fruit and cereals for breakfast. Grateful for the interruption, Abby pitched in to help.

Tripp watched Abby studiously ignore him and felt like marching over and shaking her. He'd never do that, though. Not because Julia was there, but because he knew touching her would be a mistake. Even if it would force her to tell him what she'd been up to the night before. Why she'd been sneaking around, watching him. Didn't he have enough to worry about from his own fascination with her?

And now she'd decided to ignore him. Good. He hiked the cooler higher and shouldered his way out the door. *Do your job*, he reminded himself. *She's the boss. Don't try to figure her out.* But he was worried. The fishing trip would help. He'd be out on the ocean most of the day. He wouldn't be around to watch her swim laps, to think of how his midnight swim might have been different if he'd known she was in the trees watching him. The mere thought of her, naked in the pool along with him, made him hard.

He took as long as he could to deliver the cooler to the dock. If she could ignore him, he could return the favor. By the time he returned to the kitchen with the second cooler, two of the three fishermen were drinking coffee and eating muffins. One of them, the same one who'd shown an interest in Abby the night before, was drinking coffee and talking to her.

"Why don't you come with us? It'll be fun," the man said. Then he turned to Tripp. "We have room for one more, don't we?" he asked.

Although the last thing Tripp wanted to do that particular day was be stuck on a boat with Abby while "Mr. Slick" hit on her, he kept his features neutral and nodded. Abby met his gaze briefly with a look of panic.

"Uh, no. I have some things I have to do—"

"Oh, come on. You deserve some time off," Rick continued, undaunted. "You'll bring us luck. Right, Ray?"

Ray, one of the other lawyers, moved closer to put his two cents in, and Tripp turned away.

Abby stared at Tripp's back as he opened the refrigerator to pack into the cooler at his feet the lunch Louisa had prepared the evening before. No help there. He didn't seem to have an opinion about her one way or another and for some reason that irritated her. Didn't it matter to him that they'd nearly had a naked encounter last night? Obviously not. Maybe he *hadn't* seen her...or maybe he didn't care. He probably walked around naked most the time, she decided as she watched him continue doing his job. Like he'd forgotten about the pool. And her.

Well, Abby hadn't forgotten, and she couldn't imagine spending half a day on a boat with him after—

"Surely," Rick continued, interrupting her thoughts, "living so close to the water, you must like to fish."

Abby pulled her gaze from Tripp's apparent dismissal of the whole issue and faced Rick. He was smiling that practiced smile again.

"I'm not very good at it," she said, hoping that would get *her* off the hook.

"Neither am I," he said, and the smile seemed genuine for a moment. As Tripp started past them carrying the full cooler, Rick put a hand out to stop him. "With a good mate on the boat, anyone can catch fish. Right, Tripp?"

"That's right," Tripp agreed, without looking in Abby's direction. "In the eyes of a fish, all men are equal," he quoted. Then he added his own twist. "—even women."

Rick laughed and slapped Tripp on the shoulder as he moved by them.

Abby felt like yanking down one of Louisa's professional frying pans, which were neatly hung over the stove, and using it to hit Tripp over the head. Instead, she found herself smiling sweetly at Rick. If Tripp, her *employee*, could swim naked in *her* pool at midnight and still be a wise guy, she could take up the challenge and at least act like his boss.

"Okay, I'll go," she said, and gained a little satisfaction when, on the way through the door, Tripp accidentally banged his knuckles against the frame and swore under his breath.

EVERYTHING HAD GONE fine, Tripp fumed, until Abby hooked the shark.

They had pulled away from Leah's Cay as the sky turned apricot with the sunrise. Abby had dressed in the same bathing suit she wore to swim laps. She'd covered it with a loose T-shirt but that hadn't stopped his imagination.

Tripp had purposely stayed in the cockpit of the boat, away from her, for the forty-minute cruise past the reefs and buoys to deeper water. Once they were out into the darker blue swells of the Gulf Stream, he'd let Jason, the twenty-something mate who had delivered the boat for Jimmy, take the controls.

By midmorning, the lawyers had already caught three good-size yellowfin tuna and one sailfish trolling when something struck on Abby's line with a force that nearly pulled her over the side.

Unfortunately, Tripp had been standing right behind

her at the time. He told himself that pure instinct had
made him reach for her. But as soon as he found himself
with one arm clamped around her stomach and one
hand over hers on the fishing reel, he knew he was in
big trouble. Abby, the woman he'd been fascinated
with for months, the woman he'd sworn not to touch,
was in his arms. And he couldn't let go.

"What is it?" Abby gasped as she held onto the pole
with all her strength.

"Whatever it is, it's big!" Rick said as he and the other
men reeled in their lines and the boat shifted into re-
verse to ease the pull on Abby's line.

Abby lost her footing as the fish changed direction,
and Tripp dragged her back tighter against his chest. In
the middle of the excitement, she seemed to realize their
awkward position and strained away from him.

"You take it," she said as her arms shook from the effort of holding on. "I can't do it!"

Tripp felt like shaking her. If she'd just stayed
home— "Yes, you can," he said close to her ear. "You
wanted to fish, here's your chance."

She frowned and started to say something, but the
strain on the reel jerked her arms and cut off the comment.

Tripp didn't want an argument. He wanted to put
some respectable distance between them, before everyone on the boat noticed his body's reaction to hers. "As
soon as he changes direction again and we get a little
slack, I'm gonna get you back in the fighting chair."

Abby nodded and relaxed against him slightly. Like

she trusted him. God. Tripp clamped his teeth shut on the impulse to swear. If the damned fish would just break the line, everyone would be safe...from each other.

Finally the moment came when the line slackened. In one smooth motion Tripp nearly lifted Abby off her feet as he planted her in the fighting chair positioned in the center of the boat.

"Brace your feet," he ordered. "Rick, fasten the belt."

Like a rodeo cowboy who'd just tied the hooves of a steer, Tripp had released his hold when she was secure. But the feel of her in his arms stayed with him. He'd touched her, innocently or not, and heat remained from the contact.

A long thirty minutes later, Abby, with the encouragement of every man on board except him, managed to get the fish alongside. Tripp had stayed close enough to help if she needed him, but basically watched the fight between woman and fish, while the weather seemed to change with his mood.

By the time the battle was won, and Tripp had cut the line releasing the big hammerhead, the wind had picked up and there was lightning in the distance.

Now they were racing before the storm.

Tripp turned up the volume on the marine weather channel as the boat plowed through the growing swells toward Leah's Cay. The storm was a normal late-summer squall blowing up out of the Southeast. He wasn't worried about the rain or even the wind. A boat the size of the *Miss Behavin'* could take bigger storms in stride. The problem was the lightning.

"I think we're going to get wet," Jason said, raising his voice to be heard over the wind and the engines. Braced in the cockpit next to Tripp, he looked back at the stormy horizon behind them. Just then a bright streak of lightning connected from clouds to water.

Tripp began counting—*one one thousand, two one thousand...* A loud crack of thunder reverberated around them. "You better go below," Tripp said. "No use both of us standing up here in the open." When Jason didn't move right away, Tripp added, "Check and see if any of our passengers are getting seasick."

The next spike of lightning seemed closer and Tripp started mapping the coastline with his eyes, searching for a close spit of land. He needed to find something at least as tall as they were to give the lightning other choices besides the aluminum frame of the boat's flying bridge over his head. Jason hadn't been gone for three minutes when Abby stepped up into the cockpit.

"Is everything okay?" she called as she hung on to the seat next to him to keep her balance.

Tripp shifted his gaze to her for a second. She looked worried.

"Yeah," he shouted, "we'll be fine."

In the next instant, lightning flashed again, directly over their heads, and she flinched. He wanted her out of his way, and safe. "You should go below."

She didn't move. "Are we having fun yet?" she yelled, trying to act brave.

Tripp didn't have time to trade sarcasms. In the distance he finally saw what he'd been looking for—a group of mangrove trees the size of a small island. "Hold on," he ordered and steered the boat into a hard turn in that direction.

"What are you doing?"

"Getting out of the way."

The wind seemed to die as they raced toward shallower water. Tripp didn't cut the engines until they were within thirty feet of the mangroves. It wasn't land, but at least the trees growing out of the water were almost as tall as the boat. Below them, Jason stood and looked up.

"Jason, drop the anchor," Tripp ordered before the boat had stopped moving. As the mate set the anchor and tied off the rope, Tripp turned to Abby. "Get down and find some cover before it starts to rain."

Abby didn't move. She seemed mesmerized by the thunderous black clouds rolling in off the open water. "It's so beautiful," she breathed, obviously caught by the spectacle.

Around them, the warm, thick air pulsed with an unnatural stillness. Then a blinding flash of lightning erupted from the clouds, followed by a boom of thunder so loud, it caused the boat to shudder under their feet.

It was close enough to change Tripp's mind about going below for safety. He leaned over the rail and yelled to Jason. "Get everybody off the boat."

He took Abby's arm and steered her down the steps.

Abby and Tripp reached the deck just as Jason herded the lawyers forward. "Off the boat! Any minute we might be struck by lightning. Grounded or not, if it strikes one of us, we're dead."

"Are you serious?" Rick said.

"As a heart attack," Tripp answered. "Swim for the trees. Now!" Tripp's words were punctuated by another sizzling strike of light.

Jason hit the water first, and after a startled glance, the lawyers followed. When he was sure they were all on their way, Tripp turned to Abby. He knew she could swim—he'd watched her often enough, and he didn't have time right then to explain the rule about being the tallest thing in a lightning storm. "In the water. Go," he ordered. "I'll be right behind you."

She looked toward the tenuous shelter of the trees then back at him and didn't move.

The air around them went deathly still. Giving up on words, Tripp started to reach for her but stopped. As he watched, a ball of blue light danced down the tall outrigger pole behind Abby, and her eyes widened as her shoulder-length hair rose in a cloud of static electricity. "What the—" Tripp said in awe. But he knew what it was. Saint Elmo's fire, the warning of a lightning strike. For all the sailing he'd done, he'd never seen it until now.

Time had run out. He couldn't wait for Abby to jump. With a flying tackle he propelled them both over the side and into the water.

The sound of the thunder was deafening.

Abby came up sputtering as the first big drops of rain began to fall. Then she felt a steadying hand grab the back of her shirt.

"This way," Tripp yelled, pulling her.

After a moment of shocked paralysis, she kicked into a confident swim stroke after him. By the time they neared the trees, it was raining so hard, she could barely see the boat. The lightning seemed to have passed them by, but the thunder beat like a drum over their heads.

Tripp reached the trees first and used his strength to pull her into the branches after him. That's when Abby remembered her dream. Turbulent water...strong hands reaching for her. The water wasn't very deep, but without solid ground, they could only brace between the trees and hold on...to each other. Like the dream, strong hands and safety.

A drenching rain sizzled through the leaves of the mangroves and ran down Abby's face, mixing fresh water with the saltwater on her skin and in her mouth. She felt lost in a world of water, beneath her and above.

Another flash of lightning struck, and Tripp's hand tightened reflexively on her arm. He leaned closer, bending over her slightly to block the rain. Abby couldn't see anything within three feet, but she could feel the warmth of his skin, the brush of his wet clothes, the strength in his hands. She used shaking fingers to push her rain slicked hair back and looked up into his eyes.

He simply watched her, his blue eyes as stormy as the

clouds hovering over them. Rain streaked down his skin, spiking his eyelashes and following the contour of his mouth before dripping off his chin. Suddenly she remembered him in the pool, gloriously naked...and wet. On the heels of that memory, heat ran through her, like an irrational strike of internal lightning, burning her with one thought. Maybe it was the storm or simply being alone too long. But she had to know him, to touch him—just once. And it had to be now. She might never get another chance.

Without breaking their locked gazes, Abby shifted, turning in his grip until her breasts brushed his chest and their legs intertwined. The flaring of his nostrils was the only hint that he'd noticed. But when she slipped her free arm along his shoulder and raised her mouth to his, he frowned.

"Damn," he said, sounding angry and reluctant, as though kissing her was the last thing he wanted to do.

Then his mouth took hers.

4

IT WAS A HARD KISS, a warning that she'd asked for trouble...and was about to receive it. Trouble that had nothing to do with the lightning. Or the fact that she could barely breathe. There seemed to be water everywhere—on their faces, in their eyes, in their mouths. As he swept her mouth with his tongue, she wondered if she might drown.

She didn't care.

Tripp's strong arm held her secure, an anchor in the storm, and she gave herself completely to the emphatic heat of his kiss. And to his hands. As his hot mouth engaged hers in an erotic dance of seduction, his fingers kneaded her back, then slipped to her waist under her loose T-shirt before moving upward. When Abby felt the warmth of his palm on the side of her breast, a quiver went through her. She wanted him to move, to touch her...everywhere. But he stopped.

Tripp dragged his mouth away and stared down at her as if he'd never seen her before. Like he had no idea how she'd appeared in his arms and he wasn't sure he wanted her to be there. Then slowly, as he held her with his gaze, he slid his hand up the water-slick material of her bathing suit and covered her breast.

Every one of Abby's senses instantly focused on the weight and warmth. Her eyes felt heavy; she wanted to close them, to give herself over to the primal pleasure of his touch. The patter of the rain in the leaves, the storm over their heads—everything—became a distant drumming, a thousand echoes of her own heartbeat beating frantically beneath his palm.

Don't stop. Not knowing how to say it, Abby did what she wanted to do. What her whole body cried out for her to do. She raised her arms to urge his mouth to hers once more, and as her eyes fluttered shut, she pressed her breast into his hand.

To Abby's disappointment, Tripp didn't seem to take the hint. Instead of touching, taking what she'd offered, his hand moved upward to her neck, away from her breast, and paused there as he answered her kiss. At that moment, Abby didn't have the wit or the will to complain as he ran a thumb along her chin and his lips ate at hers. When he coaxed her tongue to answer his own, she had to brace against his chest to get closer, higher.

Tripp groaned, in pleasure or defeat, she couldn't be sure, and Abby held her breath as he pushed the strap of her bathing suit out of the way and slid his hand inside to cup the soft bare weight of her breast. *Yes, finally.* She gasped into his mouth as his thumb roughly whisked the hardened peak of her nipple.

Tripp had intended to stop. As soon as he'd tasted her once, really tasted her. As soon as he'd stolen one tangible memory to satisfy his fantasies. But somewhere along the way, when Abby's mouth opened to his tongue, when she made a sound that he felt more than heard, Tripp became powerless to push her away. The rain and thunder around them receded from importance as the disturbance between them erupted with gale force.

Abby's fingers dug into his shoulder to hold on, or to get closer, and he couldn't let her go. He dragged her to his chest, then bent her backward. The wet weight of her T-shirt outlined his hand and sucked at her skin as he raised it and pushed it aside. Then his mouth found her breast, the cool puckered shape of her nipple, and the thought of stopping dropped off the horizon.

Her skin tasted salty, a mixture of the ocean and the rain. So soft and wet and warm. He sucked, using his tongue and his lips, and felt her stiffen and curl toward him. All those times he'd watched her and wanted her—now she was in his arms, willingly. Wanting him. He could feel her nails dig into the back of his neck and knew there was no turning back.

Tripp pushed the top of her bathing suit downward as far as he could under the T-shirt, and managed to free both her breasts. He guided her legs around his waist and pulled her hips close so that she could feel what she was about to receive. All he had to do was unfasten his cutoffs, pull her bathing suit aside and...

The sound of his name shattered his concentration. He wanted Abby to call his name, to scream it in pleasure. But it wasn't Abby's voice he'd heard. He held her steady and sank back into the water until they were both covered up to their chins. Then he looked for the source of the voice. He'd been so wrapped up in the moment, he'd completely forgotten where they were...and that they weren't alone.

The rain had slackened some, but visibility through the trees remained poor.

"Tripp!"

It sounded like Jason. Tripp squinted in the direction of the sound but still couldn't see him. Good. That meant he hadn't seen what Tripp and Abby had been up to.

"Yeah," he shouted. "Where are you?"

Abby squirmed in his arms, trying to get her clothes in order, but he squeezed her close to stop her movement.

"We're over here. Where's Abby?" the voice shouted. "Is she with you?"

That's when Tripp recognized the voice. It wasn't Jason, it was Rick. Of course he'd be looking for Abby. A stab of irritation ran through Tripp. Even though he knew Rick had good reason to worry about her. That didn't mean Tripp had to like it.

"She's with me. She's fine!" Tripp shouted in the general direction of the voice. Then he looked down.

Abby had begun to tremble. She gazed at him in confusion, like she'd been startled from a sound sleep and didn't know what to do. He pulled her into a hug and held her steady. He wasn't ready to let her go. The heat of her surrender was still pounding in his head and the feel of her in his arms kept him hard—excruciatingly ready to finish what they'd started.

"Tripp?"

Her voice in his ear sounded like a sigh, like a question, and he had only one answer in mind. He kissed her ear before shifting her until he could take her mouth again. She melted into the kiss as though they'd never been interrupted.

Tripp was beyond caution. If she wanted him, she was about to get her wish. He lowered one hand to cup her bottom and pull her legs around him again. Then he insinuated two fingers under the tight edge of her bathing suit at the top of her thigh.

Another tremor went through Abby, but she held on, her arms around his neck, her mouth answering his. As he slipped his hand inside the suit, Tripp heard Rick's voice again. This time accompanied by splashing water.

Tripp went perfectly still, dragged his mouth from Abby's and swore under his breath. He thought of at least three ways he could kill Mister Slick, big shot lawyer Rick. The most obvious was by drowning. *How do you save a lawyer from drowning? Take your foot off the back of his head.* Holding Abby, he rearranged her suit to its original position at the bottom, while she pulled the straps of the top into place. He knew he had to let her go. Rick would find them any moment. But he didn't like it worth a damn.

"This isn't over," he said, and even to his ears it sounded like a threat.

Abby stared up at him for a long moment, raindrops

falling on her face. She looked wary and embarrassed...and disappointed. Tripp remained still, resisting the urge to touch her again, as she brought one hand up and traced the shape of his lips with her wet fingers. Then he watched as she ran her tongue over her own bottom lip, like she could still taste him, before she nodded.

ABBY FELT as though she had a fever—burning her from the inside out. But she wasn't sick. Just hot. Tripp had touched her skin with his hands...with his mouth...and had set something off inside her. Something that wasn't going to cool down or go away until they'd finished what they'd started.

She should be afraid of this loss of control, of consequences...but she wasn't. The way her life was going, she might always be alone—just her and all the Axillar money. People believed she could have anything she wanted. Well, she wanted Tripp—without promises, agendas or lies. And if he was in the same frame of mind, she could see no reason to say no.

They'd all made it back to Leah's Cay, wet but unhurt. During the boat ride, Tripp had become businesslike and distant again, which suited Abby fine. Because every time she'd looked at him, a flush of heat—part embarrassment, part excitement—had run under her skin. She'd had to keep reminding herself to be the boss, to think about her guests.

The newlyweds had called from the airport in Miami

and were en route. When they'd arrived, she'd need to give them the standard tour and get them settled in.

But now, standing under the pounding spray of the shower, she remembered the ocean, the rain, the feel of Tripp's mouth on her breast. An inner tremor tightened her belly and a smile curved her lips as the memory of his words echoed through her. *This isn't over.*

LIFE, AS HE KNEW IT, was over, Tripp decided as he gutted the big tuna. Carlos would probably be in the mood to take a filet knife to him if he found out he'd practically made love to Abby in the mangroves...with an audience.

Tripp tossed pieces of fish innards into the water, causing the pelicans and seagulls to squabble. He paid little attention. He'd needed to work, to stay busy, so he'd volunteered to clean the fish—anything—to give him time to think with his brain instead of his libido. But his thoughts were trapped by Abby, and his body wouldn't let go of the memory of how he'd reached out to her, and how she'd come to him without hesitation. Melting to him just like she had so many times in his fantasies.

Be careful what you wish for.

His conscience remained hung up on what he'd done. He needed cool logic to override the heat he could still feel because he knew how hot it could be between him and Abby. He would bet good money the sex would be incredible. And he had absolutely no right to find out. He was there to protect her, for God's sake. Now what the hell was he supposed to do? As his hands used the knife to expertly slice along the center of the fish, he decided to stay away. She'd see the problem soon enough. And he... Well, he just needed to put a little distance between them and what had almost happened. He could do that. No sweat.

ABBY DESCENDED the staircase that evening with an air of outward calm. Several hours, and the responsibilities of running the resort, had cooled the urgency Tripp had provoked inside her, causing the trembling ache to become a singing awareness. But each step down the stairs, each brush of her soft, loose peasant skirt against her thighs and ankles reminded her that the episode was gone but not forgotten. Being in the same room with him would probably bring back the memories full force.

She felt a surge of disappointment when Rick met her at the bottom of the stairs. In many ways he was the exact opposite of Tripp. Rick's dark, perfectly trimmed hair and slightly sunburned skin spoke of a man who spent his days at a desk or in a courtroom. Tripp on the other hand was tanned and his unruly, dark blond hair was streaked with gold by the sun. Where Rick was smooth and tactful, Tripp was rough and taciturn. Remembering his gruff threat to finish what they'd begun sent another bolt of heat through Abby that culminated in a blush.

She had to get herself under control. Shaking off the

memory of Tripp, she allowed Rick to lead her into the room and pour her a glass of white wine.

"We were just commenting on the beauty of this place." He raised his glass in the direction of the other two men. "Weren't we, guys?"

"Yeah, it's a lot better than Miami, or even Key West," Ray said. "Not so crowded. If I wanted to fight traffic, I'd stay in Philly."

"The fishing is better, too," Charlie added. "And Tripp says the weather should be good tomorrow. He wants to take us to another area, farther south."

The mention of Tripp's name sent a flutter through Abby's stomach. To cover her reaction, she took a sip of the cool white wine and then gave Charlie a quick smile. "The weather changes pretty fast here because of the ocean." She shrugged. "And if you want fish, I'm sure Tripp knows where to find them."

"How long have you lived here?" Rick asked.

Abby shifted her attention back to Rick. The wording of his question bothered her. Automatic defenses kicked in. He hadn't asked how long she'd *worked* here. She shrugged off the momentary concern. She *did* live here. He couldn't know she owned the place.

"A little over two years," she answered.

"Great work if you can find it," Charlie injected with a laugh. "Where do you go on your vacation?"

Abby smiled, even though his question brought up a mixture of good and bad memories. The last vacation she'd taken had been with Larry. They'd gone skiing.

"Somewhere with mountains and snow," she answered.

"You're a skier?" Rick asked with genuine interest. "I love to ski. I know a place in Utah that's incredible."

"Hey—" Ray interrupted good-naturedly. "We're here to fish. Next year we'll go skiing."

At that moment, Louisa entered the room. "Dinner is ready," she said to Abby. "And we've set up dinner in the suite for Mr. and Mrs. Cameron."

"Thank you, Louisa." Abby smiled to herself. If she were a newlywed, she'd want to lock herself away, too.

The heat of Tripp's mouth on hers rekindled in her mind. She forced herself to return to the issue at hand, slipping back into the role of gracious host. "Speaking of fish—" she lifted an arm toward the arched doorway next to a wall-size aquarium filled with colorful reef dwellers "—shall we go eat some of what you caught today?"

The men rose and Rick fell into step beside Abby as they moved up three stairs into the dining room.

"Kay would kill me if I went skiing without her," Charlie said, continuing the conversation.

Rick pulled out a chair for Abby at the table before smirking at Charlie. Obviously the men were good friends who enjoyed harassing each other. "She's a better skier than you are. Isn't that why you married her? Because you couldn't keep up with her on the slopes?"

"Very funny—*Richard*. And while we're on the subject of being better at something...Abby outdid you at fishing today. That shark she caught had to weigh over four hundred pounds."

"Believe me, that was beginner's luck," Abby said, trying to think of a way to resign as the topic of conversation.

"How well do you ski?" Charlie persisted.

"A little better than I fish," Abby replied as Julia served the salads, and the meal continued.

After dinner, Abby pushed open the French doors that separated the dining room from a large veranda and the view of the ocean. As she stepped out into the warm, humid night, she drew in a deep breath. Her gaze automatically swept the grounds looking for a familiar figure.

The seared tuna had been delicious, the dinner conversation interesting, but she'd spent the time glancing at the doors, wishing she could excuse herself and find Tripp.

Shameless. When and how had she become so intent on Tripp? He'd been around the estate for six months and suddenly she couldn't get through a meal without wanting to see him. It had to be because he'd touched her and kissed her...and she'd seen him gloriously naked in the pool. Now she couldn't get him out of her thoughts. The onset of adolescent hormones...at age twenty-eight.

Well, at least, as a grown woman she knew who and what she wanted. She also wouldn't confuse hot sex with love. And after what had taken place earlier in the afternoon, she had a feeling she could count on everything being hot with Tripp.

She wasn't interested in love. After the Larry debacle she'd be willing to debate the existence of that particular emotion. Unless it was the love of money. Most people seemed to have a problem finding space in their hearts for another human being...but there was always a little room for the almighty dollar.

She laughed to herself.

A voice came from behind her. "What's so funny?"

Abby turned to find Rick standing in the shadowed doorway, his hands shoved in his pockets. Even though he'd asked what made her chuckle, he wasn't smiling. He looked boyish and uncertain. She glanced past him, looking for the other two lawyers. The dining room was empty.

"Nothing." She smiled, even though she was beginning to have the feeling Rick had an agenda. Again she wondered what he knew about her, and if he could possibly be harboring a crush on her money—the Axillar money. She decided to let him hang himself in his own time. "Sometimes I feel like this place is all just a dream I'm having."

Rick moved through the doorway and rested one hand on the door handle. "I can understand that. It's dangerously close to perfect." He looked toward the dock and the ocean beyond. "Want to take a walk?"

She wanted to take a walk—alone, straight down to Tripp's bungalow, but she couldn't think of a graceful way out of Rick's suggestion. "Sure," she said finally.

They stepped off the porch and meandered down the driveway, their footsteps crunching on the gravel and crushed shells as they walked. Rick made no move to touch her but strolled close enough for their arms to brush occasionally.

"So what do you do for fun around here?" he asked as they moved from the gravel onto the grass.

Not much, Abby thought, and almost laughed again. Tonight was the first time in a long time she'd actually had a plan. But she couldn't tell Rick *that*. She decided to keep the conversation professional—a resort manager talking to a guest.

"Well, there's a club up in Islamorada that has a good band on the weekends. A lot of the tourists go there because it has a bikini bar."

"Do you?"

So much for keeping herself out of the conversation. She couldn't resist a jab. "Do I what? Have a bikini? Or, go to the Purple Parrot?"

He gave her a look of exaggerated patience. "Go there."

"I've been there a few times," she said, moving away from him slightly. A movement of someone off to their left caught her attention. She glanced in that direction, and her heart began to take slow measured beats.

Tripp. Walking away as usual.

Abby watched him pace down the path toward his bungalow and wished she could escape from Rick and follow him.

Calm down.

But she didn't want to calm down. It had been so long since she'd felt like this—reckless and excited—she wanted to go for it while the heat inside her gave her the nerve.

"Is there someone special in your life?" Rick asked.

Abby curbed her erotic thoughts. Tripp disappeared from view, and she turned her complete attention to Rick.

"Why do you ask?"

He looked uncomfortable again, and he shoved his hands into his pockets once more in what seemed to be a nervous gesture. Then he stopped and turned to face her.

"I, um, I think you're an interesting woman, and I thought that if you're unattached, and I'm unattached... I thought we might get to know each other better."

Abby stared at him for a long moment. Now this was a first. She'd never been asked out by one of her guests. Even though she'd wondered earlier about his motives, he'd surprised her with his directness. The man definitely went after what he wanted.

And it looked like he wanted her...to get to know her at least. Not such an outrageous idea. Rick was certainly attractive, and he seemed like a nice guy. If she hadn't already been so tangled up in her attraction for Tripp, she might have paid more attention to Rick. But the way things were, she didn't know what to say.

"Well, I—I'm not sure what the rules are about employees dating the guests. It hasn't come up in the past. But I have a feeling the owners wouldn't approve."

Rick seemed to weigh her answer. "Would it help to tell you I know Mr. Cezare? He can vouch for me to the owners."

She should have known. Lawyers sticking together. Grumpy Cezare had probably recommended Leah's Cay to them.

"How about this?" she said finally. "I'll agree to have a drink with you sometime before you leave if Gr—if Mr. Cezare thinks it's appropriate."

Rick smiled as if she'd promised him the moon. Then, in a proprietary manner he touched her back with one hand to lead her forward. "Great."

AN EMOTION that bordered on violence shot through Tripp when he saw Rick touch Abby. Irrational on his part, but after today, he'd felt like Abby belonged to him. Rick had no right to touch her.

But neither did Tripp.

He knew he should have walked on after seeing them. He should have gone into his bungalow, tuned in to the ball game and had a beer. Instead, he'd stopped and watched, like he always did. Watching Abby was his job.

But Tripp didn't want to see Rick make a move on her. Not now, not ever. Especially after the way she'd responded to Tripp earlier. Would Rick be able to step in and finish what Tripp had started? The thought made him want to punch something.

When the front door closed behind Rick and Abby, Tripp rubbed a hand over his face and moved out into the open. He needed to step back. Maybe this was divine intervention; fate stopping him from making a huge mistake and ruining what was left of his future.

Do you want your boat back, bud? Or do you want to start over and work another thirteen years to get within six months of a lifelong dream?

He wanted his boat. He wanted his dream of sailing around the world. But he wanted Abby, too.

Out of habit, his steps took him past the pool to a spot where he could see Abby's bedroom window on the second floor of the mansion. Light spilled from the glass doors, illuminating the stone balcony and the deep purple blooms of bougainvillea draped over the railing.

He'd touched Abby, and tasted her. Part of his fantasy had come true. He needed to be content with that and let it go.

Let it go, he repeated to himself. He was wound too tight. *You need to get laid, that's all.* He thought of the on again, off again physical thing he'd had with Kelly, a woman who worked for a cruise line in Miami. They'd both been too busy for a relationship, but occasionally found time to warm the sheets. Since being at the resort, he'd been too far away to keep in touch and too preoccupied watching Abby. Maybe if he drove north and gave Kelly a call, he could head off the disaster he could sense looming on the horizon.

But when Abby's bedroom light went out, and the image of her and Rick together rose in his thoughts, Tripp knew he wouldn't call Kelly. He couldn't leave and he couldn't stay. But he had to do something or he'd end up groveling under her window like a dog howling at the moon. Or worse, climbing up to the balcony and tapping on her window like a teenager after curfew.

The thought of Carlos's disapproving expression cut off that idea.

Then Tripp wondered what Carlos knew about Rick. He almost smiled. The least he could do for Abby would be to check it out. But that would have to wait until morning, and that meant backing off for the rest of the night.

After one last glance upward, it took every bit of his willpower to turn and walk away.

5

ABBY KNOCKED on Tripp's door with a little more force the second time. She'd managed to sneak out of the house after telling Rick she was tired and planned to make it an early night. She didn't have to worry about making too much noise now. The guest bungalow where Tripp lived was surrounded by palm trees and salt bushes, a good hundred feet from the main house.

While she waited for an answer, she listened for any sign that he was inside. All she could hear were the night sounds around her, the rustling trees and shrubs, the distant whisper of waves lapping the shore.

He *had* to be there. She'd seen him half an hour ago, walking toward his place. Had he gone to bed?

"Tripp?" she called.

No answer.

Disappointed, she crossed her arms and sighed. He must be asleep. How in the world could he sleep when she could hardly sit still?

Short of throwing herself against the door and pounding, there wasn't much else left to do. She turned and walked slowly down the path. Going back to her room had no appeal; she'd only pace the floor. She might as well walk under the stars and moon.

She felt like stomping her feet or kicking something. She'd been as nervous as a teenager who'd finally decided to go all the way. And then found there was no one to "go" with.

Abby frowned and rubbed her arms. Her whole body seemed to be in high gear, revved. But she could be mature about this.... She could wait until tomorrow, or tomorrow night. She doubted if the feeling would wear off, although her patience had deserted her sometime during dinner.

She reached the turn that led to the pool, and on impulse changed direction. She didn't want to go inside and at least at the pool she could think and remember. Maybe she'd take a midnight swim. The memory of Tripp, naked, haunted her thoughts. Now that she'd touched him, been held in his arms, she wanted more.

She heard a splash and stopped. With her heart thumping in her chest, she walked forward to stand at the edge of the pool.

Tripp lost the stride of his freestyle when he saw Abby. In the dim light, wearing long loose clothing, she looked like a ghost or a figment of his imagination...of his fantasies.

Hadn't he known she would come to him? Regardless of Rick, or his own vow to stay away from the house. The male in him had known that after the way she'd responded to him during the storm, she'd come back to finish what they'd started.

Now what was he going to do about it?

He rubbed water from his eyes and stood, then he

walked forward until the water in the shallow end lapped around his bare waist. As he looked up at her, he searched for something to say to defuse the situation. A way to save them both. But when he would have spoken, Abby kept him silent by slowly pulling her loose blouse off her shoulders and dropping it near her feet. She pushed her skirt downward, then one by one, she levered off her sandals.

Tripp's tongue couldn't form words as, holding his gaze, she peeled off her panties and daringly walked naked down the steps into the water.

Suddenly, with Abby in the pool, the water, even the air felt different. Both seemed warmer, gentler, moving in currents he'd never noticed before. Goose bumps rose on his arms as his body reacted. He knew this was big trouble, but the ache inside him twisted tighter.

"Abby—" he managed to whisper.

She smiled.

Big trouble.

He put up one hand to stop her before she got close enough to touch. "Abby, we shouldn't do this," he said, almost choking on the words. In the daylight she would have seen how his body contradicted his words, but in the dark she'd have to touch him to find out.

He had to try. Although a little voice in his head reminded him that he'd resisted a woman before and still lost his business and his future. Everything but his boat, the one part of his future, of his life, he could recover. If he could just stop what he'd stupidly started... He used the hand he'd put between them to push back his wet hair. He kept his gaze on her face, stoically ignoring her bare breasts lit by the moonlight reflecting on the water.

Her smile faded, but she didn't retreat. "Why not?" she asked, looking genuinely puzzled.

Why not? Good question. Tripp couldn't tell her the truth, not just because she'd probably fire him, but because it would hurt. The very last thing he'd ever wanted to do was hurt her. She wouldn't want to know that he knew her secrets, that Carlos had sent him here to protect her and her money...from herself and men she might trust.

Trust. Damn. He'd broken his word and every trust, even to himself. And he'd lied to her. But he couldn't tell her that, either. He tried the humble approach. He could take the blame; he'd done it before. If he could stop this now, he'd at least salvage some of his pride, and Abby's, if she ever found out about him. "I, uh, today, I was out of line. I had no right to touch you." *You're the heiress and I'm the hired help.*

The smile returned, but this time more enigmatic. "Why not? I wanted you to touch me."

She took a step forward, causing him to move back into deeper water. He'd wanted to touch her—everywhere, and still did. Resisting left him wordless.

"Are you worried about us working at the resort together?" She moved closer and deeper until the water lapped around her breasts. "Is that it?"

"Yes," he hedged. Let her think whatever she wanted as long as she changed her mind. "Us, this— It's not a good idea."

For the first time since she'd appeared, Abby looked uncertain. She looked down at her hands as she sifted her fingers through the water. Her chin rose and she met his gaze. Her eyes were wide and serious. He had the feeling he wasn't going to like what was coming next.

"Tell me you don't want me...want this, and I'll leave," she said, then fanned an underwater hand toward him, which sent a caressing current of water to his chest.

Tripp sighed and shook his head. *Say it*, his conscience ordered. "I— Damn!" He had to look away. Maybe if he didn't stare into those wide questioning eyes that haunted him, he'd be able to lie convincingly.

Looking away didn't work. When he opened his mouth, the truth came out. "I want you." He looked at her then. "But that doesn't mean I have the right to take you. I would advise you to put your clothes on and go back to the house, Abby."

"Advise? God, you sound like a lawyer." Now it was Abby's turn to sigh. "I refuse to think about right or wrong. I want you. And I don't intend to go back to the house without finishing what we started today." When he didn't speak, she continued, "Look, I'm unattached and old enough to know this isn't love. I don't expect anything from you except that you keep your promise."

"My promise?"

She took another step closer and her breasts disappeared from view. In a moment he'd have to put out an arm to keep her from going under. "Yes," she said.

"You said, 'This isn't over,' and I'm counting on that."
She pushed off the bottom of the pool and slid a hand
along his shoulder.

"Damn," he said as his arm circled her as if she belonged there.

"Mmm-hmm," she answered as she brought her
mouth to his.

Abby couldn't touch bottom, but she could touch
Tripp. Somehow she'd known that if she got close
enough he'd relent. She'd never been so brazen in her
life. But she couldn't help herself. All the nervousness
and embarrassment ended when his mouth moved
over hers. His slow, reluctant giving in made her want
to sink into him, to tease his tongue with her own, to
drive him as crazy as she'd been since the last time he'd
kissed her. When he dragged her closer, and her bare
breasts brushed his bare chest, she gasped.

He held her suspended in the water and kissed her
into silence. A long, lingering kiss that clouded her
thoughts with pure sensation. She was swimming in the
familiar taste of him, breathing the scent of the ocean
and floating naked in the cool, chlorinated water of the
pool.

His hands brushed along her ribs then spanned her
waist, lifting her away from him. Her mouth clung to
his until she was forced to give way. He levered her out
of the water, exposing her shoulders and breasts to the
air and to his mouth. The storm returned.

The pleasant shocking heat of his tongue circling her
nipple arched her back. Braced by his hands, her legs

seemed to naturally insinuate themselves around his hips to hold on, bringing her in direct contact with his erection.

His teeth grazed the aching point of her nipple before his mouth covered it completely, pulling, suckling, drawing her upward into a new level of heat.

Abby wanted him to take his time, and yet, still hurry. When he moved to her other breast, an immobilizing jolt of pleasure coiled through her. She sucked in a breath and gripped the taut skin of his upper arms.

He raised his head. Their eyes met and held. Shadows and moonlight danced across the water.

"Are you sure about this, Abby?"

Abby shivered in the cool air, wanting more of his mouth, his heat. But she could feel his hesitation. He was offering her one more chance to back out. She might have smiled if she hadn't been so far gone. Tripp was definitely a puzzle. She would have guessed that he rarely hesitated about anything.

After summoning her nerve to walk down the stairs into the pool naked, Abby wasn't going anywhere. She brought her wet fingers up to his chin and lips, coaxing the tension away.

"I'm sure. Please..."

He steadied her against him then kicked toward the edge, swirling around in the water until her back was pressed to the smooth wall of the pool. The water caught between her breasts and his chest felt scalding, heated by the urgency under their skin. He kissed her—wildly, completely—and Abby dug her fingers into his shoulders to hold on.

A tiny flicker of fear ran through her. By giving him permission she'd unleashed something in him he'd been tempering. It was like offering her throat to a wolf. But even as she thought it, he eased up, moving from her mouth to her shoulder. Relief and renewed heat shot through her when he playfully bit her shoulder then sucked as he ran a hand along her inner thigh.

Tripp leaned back and held Abby immobile while he watched her face. This is what he'd wanted, what he'd fantasized about for months. The freedom to touch her, to taste her hot mouth, to hear her sigh his name when he was inside her. And he was about to have all of that, but first he needed to take his time, to drive her as crazy as she made him.

Her skin was satiny from the water, but warm. As he brushed lightly against the hair at the apex of her thighs he felt her quiver. He skimmed along her thigh once more, and she opened to him, an invitation he'd couldn't refuse or ignore.

He teased and stroked her until she clung to him with her eyes closed. She pressed her forehead against his neck, and he felt her breath coming in sweet little pants. When she tightened her fingers in his hair and breathed his name, he couldn't wait any longer.

He withdrew his hand and Abby automatically shifted her hips for more, a movement as natural as floating. It caused Tripp to break out in a sweat.

"Hold on to me," he said. His voice sounded rusty.

He cleared his throat, intending to repeat the words, but Abby had gotten the idea. She scraped her nails up his back and drew him to her.

He shoved his hands behind her shoulders to cushion her from the hard wall of the pool, then he shifted and plunged into her. Abby made a sound—of pleasure or relief, he couldn't tell—and he moved in answer. He wanted to take his time and enjoy the tight feel of her, but she seemed to have other ideas.

After several long seconds, he plunged in again. He waited, embedded inside her. His muscles ached with the urge to move. Abby's hands grew more urgent, the torment sweeter. Finally he withdrew, rushing back harder the next time. A moan escaped Abby, her fingers convulsed, renewing their grip. The water around them swirled, filled with tiny eddies of movement.

"You have to be quiet," he whispered in her ear, more as torture than truth. He didn't care if she shouted. "Shh," he taunted as he slid into her once, then, lowering his head in concentration, twice. He could feel her body tightening around him. She seemed to be holding her breath.

A third push and she stiffened in his arms. He forgot about hesitation then. He plunged into her, surrendering to the shuddering impact of her climax and his own.

Tripp held Abby for a long time...listening to her breathing and the breeze rustling the trees overhead. The water around them had calmed, but whatever had happened between them still hummed inside him. Instead of being sexually satisfied and complacent, he felt energized. Like he'd made a unique discovery. As if he'd gone scuba diving on the reef for fun and stumbled across Spanish gold.

Treasure.

Abby stirred in his arms. He kissed the side of her face. "You okay?" he asked, although "okay" wasn't what he really wanted to hear.

"Yes, I'm..." She leaned back to look at him.

Tripp's heart took several hard beats as he watched her lick her lips then smile like a satisfied woman.

"I feel much better." She laughed and then kissed him on the mouth.

Car headlights flashed through the trees from the direction of the road, causing them both to freeze. Tripp listened for a moment to the crunch of gravel as the car approached the other side of the main house. Realization of where they were and what they were doing made Tripp tighten his arms around Abby. Knowing he had to protect her from being discovered by her guests, naked in the pool, he moved backward through the water, towing her along toward the stairs.

"Who in the world could that be at this time of the night?" Abby said, sounding alarmed.

"We'd better get dressed and on dry land," he said, trying to keep his words light. Light wasn't how he felt, and he didn't want to let her go just yet. But he had no right to keep her with him and no words to explain what had happened between them. The bottom line remained; if they were caught together in flagrante delicto there'd be hell to pay with Carlos.

They stumbled up the steps together as the sound of car doors slamming echoed across the lawn. Tripp picked up his T-shirt and used it to swipe some of the water off Abby's body before they pulled on their clothes.

Still damp, but dressed in his cutoffs, he drew her to him and kissed her wet hair. "Come on."

They raced hand in hand down the walkway then across the grass to the French doors on the veranda of the big house. When Tripp pulled the door open for Abby to step through, he heard voices and footsteps approaching. The doorbell chimed.

Abby turned to look at him. She seemed torn between answering the door and wanting to say something. Tripp already knew there was nothing to say. Other than they'd both gone off the deep end in the pool. Before he could stop himself, he pulled her to him and kissed her hard on the mouth, more of a goodbye than a good-night, then stepped back into the darkness.

"DOLORES!" Abby had to press one hand over her heart because it felt as though it might pound its way right out of her chest. She needed to calm down. Surrounded by luggage, Dolores Delgado stood on the threshold with her daughter, Shannon, and Shannon's best friend, Kayla. All three looked ready to collapse. The limo driver standing behind them tipped his hat to Abby.

"I'm so sorry to barge in here this late," Dolores said as she stepped around the bags to hug Abby. "I couldn't stand that cruise one more minute. Please tell me you have room for us tonight."

"Of course there's room, Dee. Come in."

Abby glanced over Dee's shoulder and noticed that Tripp had appeared next to the limo driver. He'd put on his shirt and combed his wet hair straight back.

He glanced at her briefly, then turned to the driver. "I'll give you a hand with this stuff," he said.

The sound of his voice caused Abby's pulse to flutter faster and sent a shock wave of heat running under her skin. Fifteen minutes earlier she'd been naked in his arms and now they were standing among friends and acting like strangers. It didn't feel right, but she couldn't think of anything to say or do that would make it any better. She decided to follow Tripp's lead and stick to business. No one needed to know about her private life.

As she ushered Dolores and the girls through the door, Shannon looped her arm around Abby's waist.

"Hey—" she pulled back slightly "—how come you're all wet?" she asked with the genuine tactlessness of a teenager.

Tripp's gaze connected with Abby's as he stepped inside carrying several bags. His eyes crinkled at the corners, but he didn't smile. He seemed to be waiting to hear her answer.

"I—uh. I was taking a shower," she lied, feeling her face heat with giddy embarrassment. She moved away from Shannon, hoping the smell of chlorine wouldn't be too apparent.

"Oh, that's what I want. A nice long shower." Dolores sighed in anticipation, saving Abby from any further comment. "We left the boat in Saint Thomas and flew back to Miami. Of course the plane was late. Then the two-hour drive down—"

"I just want to sleep in a bed that isn't rolling," Shannon added.

"Well, we have your rooms ready and waiting," Abby soothed. The tired group trooped through the archway to the eastern wing of the house. They'd stayed at Leah's Cay so many times before, it wasn't necessary for anyone to show them the way.

When the bags had been divided up into the correct suites—the girls in one, Dolores in the other—and Dolores had signed the driver's receipt and given him a handful of bills, both he and Tripp turned to leave.

Abby spoke before she thought. "Tripp?"

He stopped at the door, turned to face her, and she promptly forgot whatever she'd intended to say. She only knew that she didn't want him to leave. Yet she could think of no reason for him to stay. He watched her for a long moment, his gaze like the warm brush of his hand.

Kayla's voice drifted from the bedroom of the suite, effectively slicing through the moment. "Shannon? I can't find my nightgown. Is it in your bag?"

"I'll lock up on my way out," Tripp said. And before Abby could respond, he added, "Good night."

6

SHE'D SLEPT LIKE A LOG. Or more precisely, like a satisfied woman. Physically satisfied, anyway. As Abby made her turn at the deep end of the pool the next morning, she realized how long it had been since she'd felt...truly content. Living in paradise and having money had certainly made life easier, but it hadn't brought contentment. A few things had always been missing.

Sex for one—the healthy physical expression of those hormonal urges running through her. She'd intended to learn to live alone, but she'd forgotten that there were certain things you weren't meant to do on your own.

Cutting through the water with the warm sunlight on her head, she marveled at the way her whole body felt renewed. As if Tripp's touch had caused a physical change in the way she looked at the world. Even in the way she swam laps. The water seemed to buoy her rather than resist her efforts. Swimming felt as natural as breathing.

She drifted to a stop and put a hand out to catch one handle of the ladder. She rested for a moment, feeling her heart pound from exertion. Her gaze settled on the opposite side of the pool, on the place where Tripp had held her against the wall and...

A bolt of heat ran through her, and her stomach clenched. She couldn't remember ever feeling that physical—that *sexual*—in the past. And she'd certainly never done anything like shucking her clothes and swimming naked with a man. Not even with Larry.

Her mind automatically compared Larry to Tripp. What was the difference? She'd thought she loved Larry, and yet Tripp had spontaneously released a part of her she'd never recognized before. She wasn't in love with Tripp. In lust maybe, but not love. She hardly knew him.

She wondered what Tripp thought of their midnight swim together. There had been no time to talk the night before because of Dolores and the girls. And this morning, the men had left early on the boat in search of the perfect fish. The thought of facing Tripp in the light of day ruffled her feeling of contentment.

Did what happened between them in the pool constitute a one-night stand? They weren't strangers, really, but what should they call themselves now?

Abby smiled to herself. Whatever you called it, she wanted to revel in the feeling. She wanted to—

A shadow fell across her, and she jumped guiltily, as if she'd been caught half-dressed. She squinted up into the sunlight, hoping to see Tripp. When she brought up a hand to shade her eyes, she saw Rick standing at the edge of the pool wearing swim trunks and a towel draped around his neck.

"Mind if I join you?"

"Sure. I mean, no, I don't mind," she said. "I just finished my laps."

Rick dropped his towel on a lawn chair then dove in. He came up and stopped not far from her, pushed his wet hair back and smiled.

"I thought you went out fishing," she said.

"We did. We pulled in several amberjack. Tripp took us to a great area."

With the mention of his name, the persistent memory of being in the pool with Tripp the night before rushed at her once more. Inexplicably, she felt uncomfortable sharing the same water with Rick in the light of day, even for swimming. She kept talking but moved to the first step of the ladder.

"You were catching fish but came in early? That's odd."

"Well... Charlie had a little problem with the swells, or maybe it was with the half bottle of cognac he drank last night before bed. He spent most of the trip leaning over the side." Rick moved toward her through the water as she pulled herself up the ladder. "Hey, don't leave. I may need a lifeguard." He smiled like a man willing to drown for a little of her attention.

"You swim," she said, unable to resist smiling back. "I'll watch. I've already done my laps and I want to get some sun."

TRIPP HELD HIS BREATH as he watched Abby climb out of the water. Seeing Rick with her in the pool had nearly blown the last scrap of his control. He'd already been struggling with the urge to join her in the pool himself, as if he belonged there.... Then Rick had shown up.

Tripp rubbed a hand along the back of his neck and wished he hadn't quit smoking. A cigarette seemed the only answer to calm the emotions rushing through him. The only way to ease the tightness in his chest as he watched Rick get closer and closer to Abby.

Making love to her had been a mistake—he'd known that from the first time he'd touched her. But, thinking it mattered to her would be like standing in the water fishing for sharks. It would eat him alive.

As Abby blotted her skin with a towel and stretched out on the chaise, Tripp's gaze skipped down her body, remembering how she'd felt pressed against him last night. How she'd curled around him and held on with her long, smooth legs and determined arms. Logically, he knew part of her allure had been the fact that she was out of his league, out of his reach. But after touching her, after being inside her, something else had happened. A feeling of rightness, of connection. That's what scared him. He could let her go if he had to, but he had a hunch he'd never sever that connection.

When Rick finished a few laps of the pool and moved up the stairs toward Abby, Tripp turned his back and walked away. If he didn't, he knew he'd do something he'd regret. Instead, he set off for his bungalow to do something he was supposed to do—his job. He was going to talk to Carlos. Then he would get rid of Rick.

"ABBY? Mr. Cezare is on the phone for you," Louisa called from the veranda.

"Be right there," Abby answered, hurrying through the door. The cooler air of the house made her shiver after the brilliant sunshine outside. She'd pulled an over-size shirt over her damp swimsuit but that was it. No time to change now. "I'll take it in my office, Louisa."

Abby cut through the kitchen to what used to be the housekeeper's domain before she'd taken it over. The room was small but had large windows overlooking the formal garden and Spanish-style fountain behind the mansion. She dropped her towel onto the seat of the leather chair at her desk before sitting down, kicking off her sandals and picking up the phone.

"Abby. How are you, young lady?" Carlos's distinctive Cuban accent crackled through the line.

"I'm fine, Mr. Cezare," Abby answered automatically. Even though she called him "Grumpy" behind his back, he was much too formidable and traditional to tease to his face.

"How is your business?"

"Oh, we're busy. Dolores and Shannon are here along with Kayla. We have a honeymooning couple, and of course the lawyers from Pennsylvania."

"Ah, yes. What do you think of my friend Richard?"

"Your friend? I didn't know—"

"He's a business friend, you see?"

"Oh, well... He's very nice. I think they're having a good time—catching lots of fish."

"Fish, yes. I'm sure." Carlos stopped and cleared his

throat. "Concerning Richard, I would like you to do me a favor."

"Yes, of course. What?"

"I want to invite him to dinner, here in Miami. And since I have some papers for you to look over and sign, I would like to send a car for both of you."

That meant a long drive to Miami and back, alone with Rick, and then a formal dinner with Rick and Grumpy and his wife. Abby wasn't sure she was up to it, even to be gracious to Grumpy, a man she depended on. A month ago she wouldn't have had a qualm about spending an evening in Miami. Now, after last night with Tripp, she didn't want to go anywhere. She leaned back in her chair and frowned down at her bare feet, feeling like a ten-year-old reluctantly agreeing with her father. "Well, I guess I can do that. What night?"

"I was thinking Tuesday evening. Is that agreeable? The car would pick you up at five."

A shadow fell across her desk, and Abby looked up. Tripp stood in the doorway. Her heart took several hard beats.

"Yes, Tuesday will be fine," she answered, her gaze never leaving Tripp's. "Five o'clock. Yes, I'm looking forward to it, too. Thank you. Bye."

Tripp watched Abby hang up the phone and wondered what the hell he was going to say now that he was standing in her office. He'd told Louisa he needed to speak to her about taking the sailboat out later in the week, but that had been a lie.

He'd just found out from Carlos that not only was he

not worried about Rick—the hotshot lawyer—getting close to Abby, he'd instructed Tripp to stay out of the way. In other words, Carlos *wanted* Rick to, as he put it, "court" Abby.

Tripp had listened to Carlos, the man who paid him, the man who held Tripp's dream of getting his boat back in his capable legal hands, and had felt like telling him to butt out of Abby's life. To stop trying to protect her. Stop trying to make choices for her. To let her be her own woman. Rich or not.

And do what? Let Tripp help her make choices? A man with nothing and not much chance of getting the most important part of what he'd lost back. Hardly.

So he'd kept his mouth shut. He'd given one syllable answers to Carlos's questions, then afterward he'd had the unreasonable urge to see Abby...alone.

"Come in," she said.

That was all the invitation he needed. He turned and closed the door. By the time he'd walked around the desk, she was standing. She met him partway and walked into his arms.

He tightened his hold around her briefly, then pushed her back and bracketed her face with his hands. Tripp looked down into her wide, honey brown eyes and realized that once again he was doing the exact opposite of what he should be doing. He should be telling her that they couldn't keep touching, kissing...going off the deep end.

Instead he said, "I didn't get to kiss you good-night properly," as he tilted her face upward. He watched her eyelids flutter shut, giving him permission, freeing him from all those words he should have been saying. He'd let his mouth do the talking all right. Lips to lips, tongue to tongue.

Abby whimpered when he sucked on the tip of her tongue then teased her bottom lip with his teeth. She responded with an openmouthed, tongue dancing kiss. Man, she had a great mouth. Soft and giving...and taking.

By the time he pulled back from that mouth, he had forgotten why he'd come to see her.

"I wasn't sure about what to say the next time I saw you." Abby smiled dreamily up at him. "But that was nicer than words."

Tripp pushed her hair back, away from her face and was seriously considering kissing her again when someone knocked on the door.

"Abby?"

He dropped his hands and stepped away from her as the door opened.

"Sorry. Am I interrupting?" Dolores Delgado asked after peeking around the door and realizing Abby wasn't alone.

"Uh, no," Abby said as she braced a hand on the back of her chair. "Tripp was just..."

"We were discussing taking the sailboat out on Friday."

"Yes, right," Abby ad-libbed before slipping back into her chair and scooting closer to her desk. Tripp almost smiled at her unconscious action, as if being behind a desk made her look more businesslike. Actually, she'd probably done it to put something solid between the two of them. "What can I do for you?"

Tripp watched the woman enter the room, waiting for any sign that she was suspicious about him and Abby being in the office with the door closed, but she simply went on without any discernible reaction.

"Well, I won't be a minute," Dolores promised, glancing at him before concentrating on Abby. "I was just talking to Louisa about dinner tonight and I wanted to see if we could send out for some green turtle soup from the inn. I've missed it so much. I've been having dreams about it." She smiled. "Is that okay with you?"

"Certainly," Abby said. "We'll send someone for it."

"Great. And guess what?" Dolores looked even more pleased. "Louisa is going to let me help her make the Key lime pie. I can't wait."

"That's an honor." Abby laughed. "She only teaches people she likes."

"I know. Well, that's all I wanted to ask. Thanks." She smiled in Tripp's direction. "Sorry for the interruption."

"No problem," Tripp replied.

Whether by accident or on purpose, Dolores left the door ajar after leaving, and Tripp didn't want to close it and insinuate that he expected to take up where they'd left off. Even though he wanted to. He should have never come in here. He'd avoided the main house for months. Cornering Abby in her office wouldn't do either of them any good in the long run. He wanted more.

He didn't want to have to jump apart at every sound. He wanted an uninterrupted, leisurely evening, alone with Abby—naked.

And he couldn't be sure that would ever happen.

He moved a few steps toward the door. "Guess I better get back to the dock. "I—"

"Tripp?"

"Yeah?"

Abby stood. "Will I see you later?"

The sight of her in that oversize T-shirt reminded him of the ocean, of the storm, of pulling up her shirt and—

"I, uh— Sure. You know where I live." He'd meant it as a joke but it came out sounding crass. "I mean—" He cleared his throat and confessed. "I think you know I want to see you...anytime." He held her gaze and watched color flood her cheeks. It was all he could do not to walk around the desk and kiss her again.

The phone rang. Abby ignored it.

"Will you have dinner with us tonight?"

That surprised him. The phone rang once more, then stopped but the echo of it seemed to be caught in his head. He couldn't believe his ears. "Here? In the main house?"

"Why not? We have nine people. You could round out the number."

"But I'm an employee," he hedged. And not for long when Carlos found out—especially after he'd instructed Tripp less than an hour ago to back off.

Abby lifted her chin. "I'm an employee, too. I would

like you to have dinner with us, if you want to. You can talk to the men about fish."

He took one step toward her. "Abby, are you sure I should be there? How will you explain it to the guests?"

She smiled nervously. "I'm not announcing our engagement or anything. Just come to dinner. If it doesn't go well, then we won't do it again."

Tripp felt as if he were sinking into quicksand. If this was any other woman, he could say no and not feel a twinge. But Abby... Abby already had a hold on his imagination. She was the star of every waking fantasy he'd had lately, and passing up any opportunity to share time with her seemed like punishment. But the thought of having to watch her all evening and yet act like strangers wouldn't make him feel much better. Now he truly understood that old expression about being caught between a rock and a hard place.

"You don't have to do this," he cautioned. "You shouldn't risk—"

"Trust me, there's no risk. As far as the resort goes, the more the merrier."

Tripp shook his head. It seemed like each time he tried to save them from going under, Abby pulled him in deeper. He gave up for the time being. "All right, I'll be there. But I only have so many fish stories."

Abby awarded him a sweet smile, and Tripp discovered he liked giving her what she wanted. He wished he had more to offer.

"You can tell them about the moonlight sail this weekend," she countered.

He held her gaze for several long seconds. "Moonlight...right. I could say that the best time to see it is around midnight, at the pool." He watched Abby swallow once before the corners of her mouth turned up seductively.

He took one step backward before he ended up kissing her again. "I've got to get out of here. See you later."

7

ABBY APPLIED ROSY GLOSS to her bottom lip then frowned at her reflection in the mirror. She'd left her shoulder-length hair free and, with the help of styling gel, arranged it into the kind of artful disarray her hairdresser would have approved. She'd spent more time on her makeup than usual and had tried on three different outfits before settling on a coral pink sundress that left her shoulders bare. The question now would be, why?

No mystery there—Tripp. The real question was why had she insisted that Tripp have dinner with the guests in the main house? With her?

It wasn't as though they were dating, or that she could even introduce him as a friend. Neither would be true. And a one-night stand didn't constitute being lovers.

Inappropriate lovers, maybe. Basically, he was her employee, and she had seduced him. The memory of his hesitation when she'd shown up at the pool brought a flush of color to her face and neck. How would he have reacted if he'd known she actually owned Leah's Cay? Would he have been a little more eager? She turned away from the mirror.

The wonderful, perfect, protective white lie she'd concocted to screen out her true friends from the artificial kind was supposed to take the confusion out of her life. Instead, she felt like the thing she hated most: a liar.

Tonight would probably be a disaster. But she couldn't let it go. That puzzled her. Ever since she'd witnessed that unknown side to Tripp on the dock when he'd defended her, she'd been determined to find out more. Even now, knowing so many intimate details about him—the touch of his hand, his mouth, the look in his eyes when he made love—he still seemed like a stranger. As if he wouldn't allow anyone to really *know* him.

And she wanted to know him. More than she wanted to admit. Her intentions of being alone and liking it now looked a little thin. That scared her. The last time a man had fascinated her, she'd almost made the huge mistake of marrying him. And apart from being a liar, Larry had been, on his worst day, more suitable for marriage than Tripp, the boatman.

A self-deprecating laugh escaped her as she sat on the bed and slipped on one shoe. She'd gone from sharing one dinner to walking down the aisle in thirty seconds or less. Talk about overreacting. She slipped on the other sandal and leaned back, propping her arms behind her and shaking her head.

"Get a life, Ab," she said. It had been so long since she'd been involved with anyone, she'd forgotten how to have fun. After Larry, life had become serious business.

"Well, Larry's gone," she reminded herself. And she'd survived it. Now it was time to live a little. To have Tripp or anyone else she wanted. She was glad her doctor advised her to stay on the pill after Larry left. After all, there were plenty of choices between being alone and being married. She pushed up from the bed and headed downstairs.

The formal dining room had been set for ten. Candles flickered in the center of the table amid arrangements of yellow hibiscus, violet bougainvillea and sprays of white orchids. The Mediterranean iron-and-crystal chandelier over the table had been dimmed to a muted glow.

"Everything looks beautiful, Julia," Abby commented as she circled the table.

"We are prepared to begin serving at seven," Julia replied. "Several of the guests are on the veranda having drinks. I took champagne up to the honeymoon couple. They said they would be down for dinner."

Abby moved to the French doors and looked out. Dolores sat chatting easily with Rick and Ray. Tripp was noticeably absent, as were the girls and the third lawyer, Charlie. But then, it was only quarter past six.

"When you get a moment, could you bring me a glass of Chardonnay, please?" Abby asked Julia. *I'm going to need it,* she added silently, then pushed open the doors and walked through. The sky was still bright over the water, but the heat of the day was fading. The nearly constant ocean breeze tugged at her hair and ruffled the bottom of the sundress around her legs as she closed the door behind her. The warmth felt good after the coolness of the house.

Both Rick and Ray stood as Abby approached the group.

"Good evening," she said.

Everyone greeted her, and Rick offered her his seat. Too nervous to sit, Abby declined and remained standing. She rested her hands on the back of an unoccupied wrought-iron chair and reminded herself that she was in charge here. She needed something to say. Then she remembered that earlier, Shannon and Kayla had borrowed the Rodeo to go shopping for bathing suits.

Latching on to the innocuous subject, she addressed Dolores. "So, did the girls buy anything outrageous today?"

Dolores looked up with a pained expression. "Wait till you see them. *Outrageous* is the correct word here." She shook her head in consternation. "I can't get over what teenage girls wear to the beach these days."

"Doesn't bother me a bit," Rick said with a smile. "Of course, legally, I can only look at the ones who are eighteen or older."

"Yeah, right." Ray laughed.

Rick shrugged sheepishly.

"Where are they?" Abby asked.

"Oh, Tripp took them down to the water to look at something. Kayla said she'd never seen a horseshoe crab, and Shannon wanted her to see one."

Abby glanced toward the dock and saw Tripp and the two girls huddled at one end of the dock looking into the water. He wore more clothes than she'd ever seen on him. Dressed casually in khaki pants with a black-and-cream geometric printed shirt, Tripp looked as though he'd stepped out of a country club. And he seemed perfectly at ease talking to Shannon and Kayla.

Abby had to fight a sudden feeling of exclusion. Tripp could laugh and entertain two teenage girls, yet he'd ignored Abby for months. Of course, it hadn't been necessary to laugh and entertain her.... Not wanting to go too far down that mental path, she changed the subject. "Is Charlie coming down?"

"I think so," Ray said. "He was sick as a dog and slept most of the afternoon. But I knocked on his door and he said he was going to shower and dress."

Just then, one of the girls shouted something. Then Shannon called, "Mom!"

When Abby looked in their direction, she saw the girls waving frantically, then pointing to the mangroves while Tripp stood with his hands on his hips staring up into the trees.

By the time Abby and the rest of the group from the veranda got close enough to see the problem, Abby heard Tripp's voice.

"Well, hell," he mumbled under his breath as he turned toward the dock, frowning. He headed for the boathouse and Abby looked into the trees.

Her stomach did a somersault. A pelican, tangled in fishing line, was hanging upside down from the branches. He looked dead.

Shannon and Kayla were distraught. "Mom, he's still

alive," Shannon said, tears sparkling in her eyes. As she spoke, the pelican flapped weakly, proving her words. "We have to help him."

Everyone stood transfixed, unsure of what to do. A few moments later, Tripp returned carrying a tackle box and a pair of rubber dive boots. Without conversation he put down the box, opened it and took out a knife and a pair of wire-cutting pliers. Then he sat down and pulled off his leather shoes and slipped on the dive boots.

"Now—" he looked at the girls "—even if I can get him down, he might be too injured to survive. So don't get your hopes up. He looks like a big tough bird but he's actually pretty fragile. Understand?" He waited for Shannon to nod before he squatted and lowered his feet over the concrete end of the dock into thigh-deep water.

Freeing the bird didn't take long, mainly because he was too tired to fight very much. Tripp cut the tangled web of line holding him prisoner then tucked the turkey-size pelican securely under one arm to keep him from flapping.

Abby stepped forward as Tripp placed the stunned bird on the dock. She didn't know what to do but she felt like she should help somehow. She stooped down and held the bird steady so Tripp could pull himself up out of the water.

"Okay, let's have a look at you," Tripp said like the bird could understand. There was a brief moment of contact as his hands replaced hers and Abby felt it like a shock. Tripp, however, didn't seem to notice.

Shannon and Kayla moved closer, trying not to scare the pelican as Tripp ran searching fingers over the bird's neck and wings. "He's just a big baby," he said. "See the white and yellow on his neck? That gets darker as he matures." After checking the bird thoroughly, Tripp shook his head. "He doesn't seem to be seriously injured, but he's in shock."

"Should we feed him or something?" Kayla asked, touching the gray feathers with a hesitant hand.

Tripp thought for a moment. "The best course for dealing with wild things is usually to let them go. But he's so worn-out, I don't think he could get far. How about if we put him in the boathouse for now? I'll call the Wild Bird Hospital and see what they say."

The girls enthusiastically agreed. Tripp picked up the bird and stood. Abby and the girls rose with him and for the first time Tripp seemed to realize he had an audience.

His gaze met Abby's and he almost seemed embarrassed. He glanced down past the bird feathers and dirt on his arms to the marsh mud staining his khaki pants and shrugged self-consciously. "I guess I'm going to be late for dinner."

"MOM, TRIPP SAID he'd take us to the sandbar tomorrow," Shannon announced. The girls had spent thirty minutes with him getting the pelican settled in the boathouse, and now it seemed they'd become fast friends.

Tripp raised both his hands in defense and faced Dolores. "I'll take them, but it can get a little wild out there.

They'll need a chaperon other than me. I just drive the boat."

"Mom, go with us," Shannon pleaded as she crossed the veranda to her mother.

Dolores awarded Tripp a questioning look before answering her daughter. "If you're going to wear those new suits, I guess I'll have to go."

Tripp lowered his hands in what looked like relief. Then he turned to Abby. "Hi," he said. "Sorry about the delay."

"No problem." She held his gaze, trying to read his thoughts, wanting him to feel welcome in her home. He'd showered and changed clothes since the bird incident, but he still looked a little uncomfortable. "How's the pelican?"

"The vet said to keep him quiet for the night and if he couldn't fly by morning, to bring him in to the hospital."

Abby suffered through the irresistible urge to hug him, settling instead for a momentary touch of his arm. Then she stepped back into the role of hostess.

"Shall we go in for dinner," she said to the group.

DINNER WASN'T SO BAD. Tripp made it through the first two courses without having to address the entire group. He'd been occupied by a barrage of questions from Kayla and Shannon. Since he'd become their hero by saving the pelican, both the teenagers had insisted on sitting at either side of him, and that put Abby too far away at the end of the table with Rick seated to her right. But at least Tripp could openly watch her and listen to her voice.

"Leah's Cay was built in the seventies and has been a private residence for years until recently," Abby said in answer to a question from the new Mrs. Cameron.

It was the first time Tripp had met the newlyweds. It seemed they'd spent all their time up until now in their room. Thinking about last night in the pool with Abby, Tripp decided he could understand the urge to be alone behind closed doors.

Abby's gaze shifted briefly to Dolores before she continued. "The man who owned it last died, and the house was converted into a resort again."

"Again?"

"Yes, back in the twenties and thirties when the railroad was in its heyday, there was a sizable hotel on the property. You could only reach it by boat. The rich and famous at that time used to come down to the Keys to play."

"The perfect place for a honeymoon," the new bride said, and gave her husband a meaningful smile. "What happened to the hotel? Did it go out of business?"

"No," Abby answered as she blotted her lips on her napkin. "It was blown away."

"Blown away?"

Abby nodded. "Or, washed away, by the 'no name' hurricane of 1935. They didn't start giving hurricanes names until the fifties. Anyway, some of you may have seen what Andrew did to Homestead and Miami a few years back. Well, the storm of '35 hit like Andrew, multiplied by four. It destroyed most of the railroad Flagler had built to Key West and the entire ten-story hotel on this island. The article in the Miami paper afterward talked about finding mink coats tangled in the mangroves."

"Oh, that's awful," Mrs. Cameron said.

"Have you been through a hurricane here?" Rick asked.

"No, but this house has been through a few. Nothing like the one in '35 though," Abby answered.

She'd met Tripp's gaze several times during the conversation with Mrs. Honeymooner but abruptly, after Rick's question, she focused on him. "How about you, Tripp? Have you ever been through a bad storm down here?"

With the ball lobbed in his court he tried to return it gracefully. "I was in Miami when Andrew hit," he replied, then launched into every hurricane story he could think of. He spoke to the group, careful not to mention his yacht brokerage or moving his own sailboat. Hurricanes were safe topics, especially when one wasn't bearing down on you. Talking about his personal life would only come back to haunt him if Abby got too curious. And her gaze never left him during the whole conversation, as if she intended to pay him back for watching her all evening.

In many ways for Abby, dinner went too slowly; in others it went by way too fast. Having Tripp in the room certainly made it more interesting, but being surrounded by guests kept it frustrating. As they finished dessert, the girls were busy planning the rest of the evening. They wanted to watch a new video and tried their best to talk Tripp into joining them.

When he teased Kayla about her interest in the star of the movie, George Clooney, she turned a bright shade of pink that had nothing to do with her time spent in the sun and everything to do with the man sitting next to her. Abby had to stop and remind herself that these girls were just that—girls. Obviously, one of them had a crush on Tripp, so both were determined to talk him into spending more time with them. Abby could relate to that. To his credit, he tried to fend them off gracefully by changing the subject and teasing them into nervous laughter.

As Julia cleared the dessert dishes, the guests started to rise. Abby accepted several compliments on dinner and promised a sampling of Cuban food for the next evening. In too short a time, she found herself standing with Rick, watching Tripp try to explain why he couldn't stay to view the video with Shannon and Kayla.

Finally, Dolores called to her daughter from the hall. "Shannon, leave Tripp alone. He's promised to take you to the sandbar. That's enough."

The girls looked disappointed, but they both gave in and went to watch the tape alone.

Suddenly, without room to maneuver, Abby ended up in the dining room with Rick on one side of her and Tripp on the other. Silence fell for several long seconds, then Tripp spoke.

"Well, I better get back to my place," he said, and to Abby it sounded like an intentional double entendre. *His place was not the formal dining room.* "Thanks for dinner." With a nod to Rick, he started through the arched doorway.

"Tripp?" Abby said his name before she could stop herself.

"Yeah?" He stopped but didn't turn, as if he couldn't look at her.

Excruciatingly aware that Rick stood staring at her, waiting for her to finish whatever she had to say, she felt like grinding her teeth. It was beginning to look like she'd never have a private word with Tripp.

"Is everything set for the sail on Friday?"

He looked at her, a long questioning glance before he answered. "Yes. The Beneteau is shipshape. All we have to do is stock the food and drinks on board."

"Great," Abby breathed, halfheartedly. "See you later, then." She watched his face to see if she really would see him later or if he'd simply say good-night.

His gaze shifted to Rick briefly before he said, "Okay, good-night."

Left alone with Rick, Abby tried her best not to appear disappointed. What was wrong with her? Each time Tripp walked out of a room or simply away from her, she wanted to call him back. She was being as silly as Shannon and Kayla.

Well, she refused to act like a teenager. She turned to Rick and offered him a smile. Again she wondered why she couldn't get more excited about spending time with him. He seemed like a perfectly nice guy with all the time in the world to spend with her. Unlike Tripp.

"I spoke to Mr. Cezare—Carlos—earlier today."

Rick leaned a shoulder against the arched doorway and smiled down at her. His gaze was indulgent, amused and warmer than a few moments ago. "Did you ask him about dating the guests?"

"Actually, he's invited us to dinner at his home in Miami. You and I, on Tuesday night. He said he'd send a car..." Abby heard her own voice drift into silence. Rick looked like he wanted to touch her, and she wasn't sure what to do if he did.

"I'd like that," he said. "How do you feel about it?"

She almost blurted out the truth, that she had some papers to sign and that was why she'd agreed. But Rick didn't deserve bad manners from her. "It'll be nice, although it's a long ride for dinner."

"Won't bother me a bit," he replied. "I'm on vacation."

IT TOOK ABBY two hours to get out of the house this time. The newlyweds were easy—they disappeared back to their room. Dolores, Rick and Ray were a bit more difficult. They wanted her to share after dinner drinks with them. The last two days had given her several reasons to wonder why she'd ever wanted to run a resort in the first place. What was normally an enjoyable, gracious atmosphere to get to know people and share their interests had become *work*.

For the first time in a long time, she wanted her own

time to play. She also had to find a way to explain to Tripp, before it came up in casual conversation, why she was going to Miami with Rick. Not that she owed him an explanation, she reminded herself. She didn't. But it seemed only fair to talk to him about it. In case he wondered. So, after escaping the group on the pretense of making some phone calls, she'd changed into a pair of linen shorts, pulled on a sleeveless silk blouse and sneaked out through the back courtyard. She was well on her way to Tripp's bungalow when a hand shot out from the darkness and stopped her.

Tripp covered her gasp with his mouth and kissed her until she kissed him back. Then, without releasing her arm he said, "Let's get out of here."

Without words, she let him lead her to his Jeep and moments later they were flying down the bumpy, crushed shell-and-gravel road toward U.S. 1 and civilization.

THIS IS REALLY STUPID, Tripp admonished himself as he turned onto the main road. He shouldn't have kissed her, but after watching her mouth all evening—from a distance—he'd given in to the aching urge to taste her.

Earlier, sitting at the dinner table, he'd decided that if she came to him, on her own, he'd get her out of there, take her someplace away from Leah's Cay. To make a run for neutral ground, where no one knew them and no one cared whether they talked or touched. He reached over and covered her hand with his.

"Where are we going?" she asked, sounding breathless.

"Anywhere," he answered.

She nodded in agreement.

Out of habit, several miles down the road, he turned into the crushed-coral parking lot of the Pelican Bar.

"This okay?" he asked. "We can sit outside. It shouldn't be too noisy."

"Fine."

They entered the cool dimness of the bar and were immediately assaulted by the smell of spilled beer and the loud strains of Jimmy Buffet singing on the jukebox. Tripp began to think he'd made a mistake coming here. He was sure Abby didn't frequently hang out in a bar that could barely claim the title "rustic." The contrast between Leah's Cay and a dive like the Pelican made him wince. It graphically illustrated the difference between his life-style and Abby's. He stopped, thinking he'd take Abby somewhere else when a waitress wearing a T-shirt and neon orange short shorts passed them, carrying a tray. She had to raise her voice to be heard over the music.

"Hey, Tripp." She looked Abby over briefly then waved them toward the big open room. "Sit anywhere you like." She started to walk away, but Tripp touched her arm and stopped her.

"How about outside? Is there any room out there?"

"Yeah, I think so. That's Deb's station."

Just then someone at the bar yelled for another beer

and accented the request by throwing a plastic fish at the bartender. "What are you? Deaf?"

Knowing the bartender and his probable reaction to the drunk at the bar, Tripp took Abby's arm and steered her toward a doorway covered with heavy plastic panels that parted like a beaded curtain. He had to almost pull her along, she seemed mesmerized by the ceiling and the walls of the Pelican. Nearly every square inch was covered by snapshots, pinned up, stapled up, taped up.... A veritable wallpaper of fishermen and their fish.

He tugged her through the door just as the bartender threatened to make the drunk at the bar eat—without the benefit of knife and fork—the particular fish he'd just tossed at him.

Outside, the noise level dropped. The ceiling fans above each table churned the air, and the pungent smell of the marsh at low tide mixed with the distinctive tang of diesel fuel managed to overpower the smell of stale beer. They had a choice of two built-in wooden tables at either end of the wide porch that extended over the water of the marina. Tripp chose the one farthest from the door. It offered a little more privacy, and the chance to feel the breeze off the ocean. He seated Abby with her back to the bar and the other tables, then scooted in opposite her.

"Alone at last." Abby smiled.

"Yeah," Tripp answered, "with just twenty or thirty of our closest friends."

"That's the point, isn't it? No one knows us here."

"Well, they know me—" he waved to get the attention of the waitress "—but they don't care about who I'm with."

Abby started to comment but the waitress arrived. After placing their order, they were left alone. And suddenly Tripp couldn't think of a damned thing to say. He needed to tell her that they had to stop what they'd started. He wanted to tell her that he knew everything about her, even the fact that Rick intended to "court" her, as Carlos put it. He had to tell her the truth. But he hadn't quite decided how to accomplish that.

"Isn't that Jimmy Rittner's boat?" Abby asked, as if she couldn't stand the silence.

Tripp gazed out toward the water and found the *Miss Behavin'*, third in the line of ten or twelve boats docked there. "Yeah."

"How long have you two been friends?"

It was a simple question, yet he was so used to keeping secrets that he didn't know how to answer. He tried part of the truth.

"We're not really friends. I met him in here a couple of months ago and we got to talking."

"Oh."

She didn't seem satisfied with his answer. "Why?" he asked.

"I don't know much about you, what you do when you're not at the Cay. I thought talking about your friends would be a good start."

If you knew about me, you'd probably hate me. I need you

to get my boat back. "There's not much to know really. I spend most of my time working or at the guest house."

"How long have you lived in the Keys?" she persisted.

Too long. "Uh, since I started working for you—I mean, the resort."

She kept looking at him, waiting.

"I lived in Miami before that, for about twelve years."

"Where did you work in Miami?"

Time to change the subject. "What is this? A job interview?" He smiled when he said it, but still color moved up her neck and into her cheeks.

"I'm sorry. I—"

"No harm, no foul." He felt lower than a sea slug. Manipulating her with her own good manners left a bitter taste in his mouth. Tripp saw the waitress push through the door with their drinks. "Tell you what, ask me again after a couple of beers. You never know what will happen."

The harried waitress came and went. And as Abby took a sip of the Pelican Bar's world-famous "Margaritaville" margarita, Tripp couldn't resist a return volley. He took a long sip of his beer and said, "So what's your favorite thing about Leah's Cay, besides the pool?"

He felt a twinge of conscience when she choked on the margarita and started coughing.

"Are you trying to kill me?" she squeaked as her eyes watered and she drew in a breath to regain her composure. She carefully set her drink down and gave him a stern look.

He himself almost choked, from laughing. He couldn't help it, Abby looked so ticked off. Then something miraculous happened.

She started laughing with him.

When the worst of it died down, Tripp handed her a napkin to wipe her eyes. "You rat!" she said without any anger as she snatched the peace offering. Then she smiled.

That's when Tripp realized he was flirting with her. It had been so long since he'd actually wanted to make a woman laugh, he thought he'd lost the skill. Or maybe the will to even try. He'd been too busy trying to put his life back together after his partner's ex-wife had gone through it like General Sherman with a blowtorch. Come to think of it, *she'd* smiled through the whole process. No wonder he'd given up on entertaining women.

He watched Abby dab at her eyes then crumple the napkin, and he felt another twinge of foreboding. She wouldn't laugh when she found out the truth about him. And he couldn't let her or himself get in too deep before that happened. And it *would* happen.

Tripp stared into Abby's wide eyes, watched the wind toss a few strands of hair across her mouth. When she brought one hand up to tug the strands back behind her ear, he covered her other hand with his and tried to find the right words.

"I feel like I should apologize," he said.

She looked surprised. "Why? I lived through it."

"No, I mean—" He pulled her hand closer and used both of his hands to lazily investigate her fingers. "For getting us into this, I guess."

Abby blinked once then she went very still. "Into what?"

He held her with his gaze. "For what happened between us at the pool."

"Why should you apologize? I wanted it to happen as much as you did." She looked away for a second then back. "Maybe more."

After hearing that piece of honesty, he had to stare down at their intertwined fingers in order to say what needed to be said next. "I doubt that. But in any case. I was wrong. We... What happened that night was—" He couldn't help it; he had to look her in the eye and let her see one little portion of the truth in him. "It was incredible."

He watched the effect his words had on her, the slight flare of her nostrils and the softening at the corners of her mouth. She looked like she wanted to be kissed, and by him. Right now. He forced his gaze down again.

"But it can't happen again. We can't—"

A vibration of something pounding the wood at their feet jarred the seriousness of the moment. Then a voice boomed, "Tripp! Yo, Tripp!"

Tripp wanted to swear when he saw the infamous Captain Jimmy Rittner thumping his way toward their table on his crutches instead of a peg leg. Tripp glanced at Abby and shrugged in apology, but he felt helpless.

When Jimmy reached them, he dragged a chair from

several lined against the opposite wall of the building and sank onto it at the end of their table. Without preamble he tossed his crutches to the floor and blurted out, "Tripp, they're takin' my friggin' boat."

8

JIMMY PROPPED HIS ELBOWS on the table and scowled like a pirate searching for blood to shed. As an afterthought, he nodded to Abby. "Hi."

"Hello," she answered carefully, as if she'd just as soon stay out of this conversation.

Tripp barely noted the exchange. He was busy with damage control. The night he'd told Jimmy about his own boat and his fight to save it was fuzzy in his memory. It had been months ago. He'd been in a dark frame of mind and had downed enough tequila to feel like talking to someone. Now his weak moment was about to bite him back, through Jimmy.

"I got served today. I have to be in court on the twenty-first."

Both Jimmy and Abby were looking at Tripp, waiting for a comment. The best he could do was "How much do you owe them?"

"Not enough for them to take my damned boat," Jimmy answered angrily. "I want to know that lawyer's name. The one in Miami, the one who's getting your boat back."

Tripp wondered whether he could save the moment if he just hauled off and punched Rittner out of his chair, then escaped with Abby. He doubted it. Punching Jimmy would merely tick him off, not make him shut up.

"I know a lawyer—" Abby glanced at Tripp looking unsure "—in Miami. I could ask him to—"

"Whoa. Wait a second," Tripp interrupted. He turned to Jimmy and gave him a meaningful glare. "Jimmy doesn't need your lawyer. And we don't need to talk about this right now. I'll be glad to give him the name and number of mine—later."

"Great, man." Jimmy looked relieved, but he'd missed the hint to shut up. "If I can stall 'em for a while, maybe I can come up with the money. That's what you're doing, isn't it?"

"Sort of," Tripp answered. Abby's gaze made him twitch inside. She'd stopped asking questions about Tripp's past but they were still there, drifting between them like smoke.

"You know, Tripp, we have three lawyers at Leah's Cay. You could ask one of them," Abby suggested. "Isn't there some kind of law that says you can't obstruct a person's right to make a living?"

Yeah, right, Tripp thought bitterly. If that were true, then he'd still have his half of a successful yacht brokerage...and his sailboat. And the thought of Abby bringing Rick into this made the beer he'd just drunk feel like acid in his stomach. He'd rather walk barefoot on a bed of sea urchins.

He took another mouthful of beer before he answered in such a way it would seem like he was considering her option. "As far as I know, anything you own is fair game in a lawsuit," he said finally. "Besides, the guys at the resort are from out of state. I don't think they can advise on Florida law."

Damn. Abby was watching him again, waiting. He needed a way to change the subject. Any kind of distraction would do. Out of the corner of his eye he spotted the waitress and waved to her. "Hey, man, looks like you need a beer," he said to Jimmy.

After they'd ordered, Tripp gave it his best shot. "Did you watch the Marlins game?"

THE THREE OF THEM walked out of the Pelican Bar an hour later, and by that time, Abby knew more than she ever wanted to know about baseball. Jimmy escorted them to the edge of the gravel parking lot, crutches and all, before he reluctantly said good-night. As if he didn't want to be left alone.

After living at the resort two years without a good friend to talk to, Abby could understand that feeling. Tonight however, she'd wanted to be alone with Tripp, and Jimmy had elbowed his way into their evening. Now they were on their way back to Leah's Cay and she felt a sense of urgency to get something, anything, straight between them.

Except that when Tripp started the Jeep, he switched on the radio. And he seemed to look anywhere but directly at her. Finally, five minutes from home, she couldn't take it anymore.

"Would you pull over, please?"

"What?"

"Pull over."

As Tripp slowed and turned into a roadside stop next to one of the many bridges, he asked, "Are you okay?" They stopped so quickly, dust from the gravel shoulder caught up to them and swirled around the Jeep. He left the engine running. "What's wrong?"

Instead of reaching for the keys and turning off the engine like she wanted to do, Abby opened her door and got out. She walked through the bright illumination of the headlights, away from the Jeep, and waited. Purposely ignoring him, she stared out over the water for one long moment before the Jeep's engine was shut down, the lights switched off. She heard the sound of Tripp's footsteps approaching her slowly, as if he wasn't sure he wanted to get too close.

"Abby?"

She turned to face him. She wasn't sure what she wanted, either, except more. More about him, more with him. Just more. She gazed up at his shadowed features and remembered him in the dark, in the pool. A shiver ran through her, and she rubbed her arms. She wasn't cold; she was in danger of melting.

He'd told her that what had happened between them had been an "incredible" mistake. She had to test the truth of that statement. To see if he really meant it when he said it couldn't happen again.

"Did you mean it?"

He balanced his hands on his hips and looked confused. "Mean what?"

"When you said what happened between us the other night was a mistake. Did you mean that?"

He looked away for a moment. The darkness prevented her from seeing the intense blue of his eyes, but his features were tense, almost angry.

He crossed his arms and met her gaze. "Yeah, I meant it."

"Why? You said—"

He put up a hand to interrupt. "Abby— I...like you. I— Damn." He rubbed the back of his neck as if to ease the tension there before he spoke again. "We were together one time. It can't become a...thing. You know what I mean?"

"A thing? You mean a regular thing? An affair?"

Tripp stepped forward and gripped her shoulders as if he meant to shake her. "Listen to me. Don't make this into something it isn't."

He didn't have to shake her. The feel of his warm hands on her bare arms jolted her from the inside out. She stared up at him, ready...wanting to step closer, to be held. But after one drawn-out pause, he suddenly let her go.

"Look at you," he continued. His gaze ran over her from head to toe. "Dressed in your linen and silk." He gestured impatiently. "You live in the big house. You run the whole place. And me?" He dropped his hand. "I am what you see. I run the boats, take rich people out fishing."

Abby felt breathless, as if every bit of air had been sucked out of her lungs. She wanted to disagree, to ar-

gue that he was more than that—something inside her
knew it. He was smart, competent and too controlled to
be a convincing boat bum. But he'd derailed her by his
rejection. He didn't want to touch her, to be with her,
even though she was willing. What did that say about
her feminine appeal?

Then she remembered Larry, who'd only pretended
to want her for the money. He'd damaged her self-
esteem in a big way and it had taken her two years to recover. At least she didn't have to worry about repeating
that scenario because she'd learned how to pretend.
Tripp didn't know about her money, due to her own lie.
Nevertheless, he was saying he didn't want her because
he was the boatman and she was the boss. It was
enough to make a grown woman want to stomp her feet
and scream.

"So you're worried about your job," she said, a statement rather than a question.

Tripp drew in a deep breath and let it out before answering. "Look, I moved down here to simplify my life.
And when I think of you and me, all I see are complications."

Abby had to concede. He was right. She'd already
witnessed the complications firsthand. The whole thing
between them was a bad idea, but that didn't mean it
didn't hurt to have him point it out.

"I understand," she said, and made an attempt at a
real smile.

"What?" he asked.

He seemed so perplexed, she almost felt sorry for

him. But right now, as wealthy as she was, she couldn't afford pity. She had to take care of herself, to avoid falling into the "I'm not the perfect woman trap" again. If nothing else, she had to remember she had options.

"I understand what you're saying." She swallowed to ease the tightness in her throat, and used his earlier words. "No harm, no foul. I just wanted to get everything straight between us because I'm going to Miami on Tuesday night with Rick and I wasn't sure how you'd feel about it. Well, now I know." She shrugged in what she hoped looked like indifference and started back to the Jeep. She had to put some space between them and take a few moments to recover. The evening had turned out so differently than she'd imagined, she felt like crying.

She climbed into the Jeep, closed the door and looked out of the windshield. Tripp still stood in the dark where she'd left him. His hands were on his hips again and he seemed to be studying the gravel near his feet. Finally he shook his head before walking back to the driver's door. Without another word, he slid into the seat, started the engine, shifted into gear and threw gravel with the tires as he returned to the road.

TRIPP SAT in the Jeep for a long time after Abby went into the house. *Welcome to the world of doing the right thing*, he thought bitterly. A world where someone else—like Rick—gets what you want. And you stand by and let her go. He closed his fingers into a fist and thought seriously about hitting something. But as he stared out the windshield toward the ocean, a surge of resignation rolled over him. He had no choice. He'd given his word to protect her from unsuitable men—like himself—and even though he'd slipped up, he could make it right by letting it go. Letting Abby go. He sighed, opened the Jeep door and got out, then satisfied his anger by slamming it soundly.

Tonight was Sunday night. He had two nights to think about what would probably happen on Tuesday. He knew what Rick wanted...and he knew how Abby could respond. Especially now that he'd cut her loose. She'd be ready for Rick, because instead of giving her any reason to say no, he'd practically shoved her into the lawyer's arms.

Thinking of the two of them together created more pain than he wanted to feel. Tripp decided to get drunk. He had an unopened bottle of Cuervo in his cabinet. Maybe he'd pass out and wouldn't have to think about what it had cost to do the right thing.

A BRILLIANT FLASH of lightning and the rumble of thunder that followed it opened Abby's eyes. She'd been drifting off, finally, after tossing and turning for what seemed like hours. She glanced at the bedside clock glowing green in the darkness—2:32. Tripp had brought her back to Leah's Cay around midnight. After showering and slipping into a gown, she'd still been too upset to sleep. So she'd paced her room for almost an hour before flopping down on her bed in exhaustion.

The wind picked up outside, causing the plants near

her balcony doors to scratch at the glass. Another flash of lightning lit the sky and the first drops of rain hit the windows.

The weather reflected the way she felt inside. Stormy, turbulent, confused. She refused to cry, however. What happened between her and Tripp wasn't the end of her world. She hadn't had time to fall in love, she'd just fallen in lust...hadn't she?

Abby balanced the back of one wrist on her forehead and studied the dim shape of the ceiling fan spinning above her. To her complete humiliation, tears formed in her eyes. Even though she would admit to being intrigued by him for some time, she couldn't be in love with him. She didn't even *know* him. Wiping a trail of moisture away, she clamped her teeth tight and resisted the urge to sob into her pillow. He'd just hurt her feelings, that's all. And she—

Outside, the rain fell and the wind blew something against her balcony door. Abby glanced in that direction as a flash of lightning illuminated the glass panes. Her heart nearly stopped, freezing her in place. Someone was standing on her balcony. She heard a knock and the sound of her name before the knob turned and the door swung open.

In one heart-pounding moment, she realized it was Tripp.

9

THE WIND-DRIVEN RAIN followed Tripp inside Abby's room, pattering on the rug, twisting the sheer curtains. Standing half in and half out, he seemed lost, surprised to be there.

As Abby untangled herself from the sheets and stumbled from the bed, Tripp took a step backward.

"Tripp!"

He stopped at the sound of his name.

Lightning blazed from cloud to cloud above the trees and everything in the room froze in the brilliance. Abby could see him clearly. Wearing only a pair of dark cut-offs soaked by the rain, he looked like he had that night she'd watched him swim in the pool. Except for his face. His features were set, the hard line of his mouth communicated danger. If he'd been a stranger, Abby would have been terrified.

But he wasn't a stranger. Not anymore. And she wanted to touch him, to bring him inside. To smooth away his anger. As if he'd read the welcome in her eyes, in her voice, he shoved the doors shut, closing out the storm behind him.

His breathing sounded loud in the darkness. A second later, his hands were on her, dragging her to him.

The moisture on his chest soaked through her thin gown as his mouth closed over hers.

The kiss started out hard, almost painful, but she didn't struggle. Dimly she felt him shove his fingers into her hair to keep her still. Like he was afraid she'd run if he didn't.

She wasn't going anywhere. To prove it, she skimmed her nails over the wet, bare skin of his back and held on. Tripp drew in a sharp breath and hesitated in the ravagement of her mouth. When he exhaled, his lips softened and his intent seemed to change. Hard and angry became slow and wet.

The change was devastating. Abby had wanted him, even in anger. But as one searing kiss melded into another, heat slithered downward, making her breasts ache and her knees weak. She heard a low, yearning whimper and realized it had issued from inside her. Her body was pleading for what Tripp could give her, with his mouth, his touch.

Tripp recognized the sound of surrender. He could feel it on her warm skin, taste it in her soft, hot mouth. When he'd stepped into her room, he'd half expected to be thrown out. He deserved it. No way should he be here. But he was, and now after touching her, after feeling her response, he couldn't leave. Not until he'd been inside her and felt her explode around him. Not until he'd given her something to remember on Tuesday night when 'slick' Rick put the moves on her.

Tripp delved into Abby's mouth again, teasing her with his tongue and teeth. He wondered if she could taste the tequila and lime. His attempt to get drunk and forget had backfired. The tequila had simply taken the edge off his conscience and made him reckless. Now he was lost.

They were both lost.

Abby shivered and arched her soft breasts into his chest, teasing him with the silky feel of her gown and the hardened tips of her nipples. He didn't want any more tequila, he wanted Abby.

Without relinquishing her mouth, he led her to the bed, then sat on the edge. Instead of pulling her down with him, he kept her upright with his hands on either side of her rib cage. He drew her closer, between his knees and kissed her belly through the wet silky material of her gown. Then he nuzzled the underside of her breast, inhaling the smell of the rain-dampened material, the fragrance of her warm skin. He could spend the night breathing her in and...

He licked the thin silk over her nipple, then sucked.

A moan escaped Abby. Her head dropped back, exposing, offering. Her fingers gripped his shoulders, but she didn't move. He used his tongue and the wet material to tease one nipple then the other until she seemed to be teetering, melting. He slid her panties down and off, then relaxed backward. Lying on the bed, he drew her forward to straddle his hips.

He pushed vertically once, grinding into her to placate the ache of his erection. But he wasn't ready to give in to it yet. He slid his hands along her thighs and around to grip her bottom. In tune with his movements,

Abby raised her hips slightly to give him access. With one strong pull, he dragged her upward. She gasped and lost her balance but ended up with her knees on either side of his head—exactly where he wanted her.

Abby wasn't sure what she'd expected...but this wasn't it. Her first instinct had been to pull away, but Tripp held her steady, forcing her to wait breathlessly to see what he would do.

He started with simple kisses, light and butterflylike on her inner thigh. His warm breath teased her most intimate parts as his tongue traced small figure eights over the skin he'd just kissed.

If he'd grabbed her and been rough, Abby might have resisted. But as Tripp's fingers slid lightly from her bottom to the small of her back, leaving goose bumps in their wake, her arms trembled with the rush of sweet pleasure. She couldn't move, it felt so...good.

Then Tripp kissed her deeply, there, between her thighs, and she nearly collapsed. She had to put her head down and twist her fingers into the bedcovers, to concentrate on keeping her arms straight, holding herself upright. Otherwise she'd miss what was coming next. And she wanted whatever he intended to do to her.

She gripped the sheets and whimpered as his tongue delved deeper, as her body answered by growing wetter. Outside, the storm was passing, thunder and lightning moving away. Inside, the turbulence remained, swirling through her body, making her quake with scintillating pleasure.

Tripp.

Just as she thought she couldn't take any more without flying into a thousand pieces, he relented. He pulled back, teasing and kissing her thighs as he'd done in the beginning. For Abby, now that she'd danced on the precipice, teasing wasn't enough. She wanted Tripp, all of him, inside her, urging her over the edge.

She backed away, intending to scoot down, but in a sudden, smooth motion Tripp reversed their positions. Abby, on her back now in the center of the bed, watched as he rose to his knees and unfastened his cutoffs. He pushed them down, kicked them off, then loomed over her. One of his hands shoved her gown up, and for the first time he seemed impatient.

"Let's get rid of this," he muttered as he yanked the gown over her head and dropped it behind him. Then he worked his way upward, kissing her thighs, rubbing his face against her belly.

Abby refused to wait any longer. She couldn't. He'd ignited the fuse, now she needed the explosion. With eager hands she coaxed him higher, closer. When he stopped to tease her nipples briefly, she couldn't keep quiet.

"Tripp, please—"

But he didn't comply. Caged by his arms she remained ready, willing, and...empty. In agitation, she brought one knee up and wrapped a leg around his hips. She felt his arms quake in response, holding back.

"Tell me you want it," he said harshly. "You want *me* inside you."

"Yes," she breathed, arching her back. "I want...you. *Please*. Tri—"

Tripp couldn't wait anymore. At her yes, he'd pushed forward. By the time she said his name, he was buried deeply in her softness, surrounded by and surrendering to her heat. Whether it was the tequila or the original thought of giving her up, a steamy fog seemed to fill Tripp's mind. He drove into her again, and again, marveling at the way her body answered his, thrust for thrust. A perfect fit.

He lowered his head as her fingernails sank into his backside. The warming tickle of her breath shimmered along his neck. Then she made a pleading sound and he couldn't think, he could only move and feel. He increased the pace—harder, faster. *Hurry, baby. I need to hear it, to feel it. Before I go crazy.*

"Do it, Abby. Give it to me."

He couldn't tell if she'd heard him, he'd barely been able to force the words out. But she moaned, apparently lost in the excruciating friction between them. The next few strokes sent her over the edge. Abby curled into him with a provocative cry of release. As the pleasure overtook her, Tripp came in a sudden, shattering climax that nearly immobilized him.

When he could move again, he rolled from her, but one arm remained trapped under her shoulder, his fingers still tangled in her hair. Abby turned, snuggling closer. She tried to speak but he shushed her.

He had no words and he didn't want her to think she had to say anything. In the last half hour, they'd an-

swered all the questions that needed answering tonight.
The rest could wait.

Now he knew what her bedroom looked like from
the inside, what it smelled like—Abby. For several
minutes he listened to the rain tapping against the glass
in the balcony doors, and enjoyed just being there.
Abby grew so still, he thought she'd drifted to sleep.
But when he moved, she spoke.

"Are you leaving?"

"No. Be back in a second." He levered himself up off
her bed and walked through a door he hoped would
lead him to the bathroom.

Relaxed and replete, Abby could barely keep her eyes
open. But she didn't want to go to sleep yet. She wanted
to enjoy the aftermath of what had just happened. Hot
sex. The hottest she'd ever experienced. And something
beyond sex. A yearning. She wanted Tripp to stay with
her, to sleep with her, to share something else beside
their bodies. Yet she had the feeling that if she went to
sleep, she'd wake up alone.

Abby heard water running, saw the light switch on
and off again. Tripp returned from the bathroom with
something in his hand. He kissed the side of her face
then placed the warm, wet cloth on her belly before rubbing it downward, between her legs.

A raging flush of embarrassment enveloped her.
She'd never known a man like him. One minute he was
shoving her clothes out of the way, the next he was
gently washing away the aftermath of their joining. She
couldn't speak, she could only lie docile, turning this

way or that as he indicated. Satisfied, he made one more journey to the bathroom before he returned, pulled the sheets back for her to slide underneath, then crawled into bed next to her.

There was so much she didn't know about him. He'd explored all the secrets of her body and yet he remained a stranger. But she was hesitant to ask too many questions. When she'd tried to earlier he'd deflected her. He'd told her he wanted to keep his life simple, to keep his job. Yet here he was, in her bed. She couldn't resist teasing him. Yawning, she cuddled closer and brought her lips to his ear.

"You're fired," she whispered.

His movement stilled, mid-cuddle. But Abby couldn't hold her serious act. She laughed and he growled in answer before squeezing her until she gasped for breath.

"Go to sleep," he ordered. "You can fire me tomorrow if you feel that way about it."

With his arms around her and a smile on her face, Abby closed her eyes and obliged.

Tripp watched Abby drift off like she didn't have a problem in the world, and he fervently wished he could make that statement true. He hadn't been able to stand the thought of her being with another man, with Rick. But, by coming to her, he'd just multiplied all their problems tenfold. Making love to her once could be considered a crime of passion, a lapse of judgment. Twice meant his judgment was down for the count, knocked out by his obsession with Abby. And now she knew it.

He pushed up on to his elbow and looked down at her. Here she was, lying trustingly in the arms of a man who was supposed to be protecting her from men who would use her and hurt her. He was worse than any stranger. From now on, whatever he did would ultimately hurt her. Because he couldn't tell her the truth.

Carlos had told him how her fiancé had lied about everything. And Tripp remembered once when Larry's name had come up in a conversation between Abby and a guest. He hadn't been a part of the conversation, but he'd seen the way her face closed up, the pain quickly hidden.

He was as bad as Larry, or worse. He should get out of her bed once and for all before he did even more damage. But when he slowly pushed the covers down in order to slip out without waking Abby, she stirred in her sleep as if she'd read his intent. Her arm coasted along his chest and one of her legs slid over his. She looked so peaceful, he hated to disturb her. And apart from knowing that he'd have to pay the price for his own growing feeling of contentment, he wanted to enjoy her for as long as he could. He relaxed back on the pillow and pulled Abby closer. He'd just stay for a little while.

SHE WOKE UP ALONE.

Abby opened her eyes and turned on her side. The sheets around her were rumpled, the white lace duvet kicked off onto the floor. And she was naked. Tripp had been there. It hadn't been a delicious dream. She yawned, then ran a hand over the pillow next to hers. The last thing she remembered was him pulling her back against his chest, holding her with a possessive arm. Whispering, "Good night."

Now he was gone. Without waking her, he must have slipped out the way he'd come in, over the balcony. And she missed him, even though as she stretched and closed her eyes, she could almost feel his hands on her again. She smiled at the thought of simply staying in bed, naked, until he came back to her. Or not.

Glancing at the clock she jumped when she saw the time. Nine-thirty. Breakfast was well underway. As she pushed the covers back and got up she wondered what everyone thought about her absence. Then she decided she didn't care.

After taking a shower and getting dressed, she headed downstairs. The house seemed empty. Determined to find coffee, Abby discovered Dolores in the kitchen, drinking a cup and chatting with Louisa, the cook. Everyone else, it seemed, had somewhere else to be.

"Good morning," Dolores said in an inquisitive tone. "Are you feeling all right?"

"Fine," Abby answered as she poured herself a cup of coffee. Then to Louisa, "Breakfast went well? No problems?"

Louisa filled her in on the guests. "The honeymooners ate early in their room. The lawyers are playing tennis, and I believe the young ladies are at the pool."

"Tripp and the girls set the pelican free this morning, and he flew away. So it seems he recovered from the ordeal," Dolores added.

"Great. Looks like this place gets along fine without me." She was glad to hear that the pelican would survive, but it was the mention of Tripp's name that made her heart pound. *She* hadn't completely recovered from the night before. To cover her reaction, Abby moved over to the commercial-size refrigerator and opened the door. "I'm starved," she said as she removed a carton of eggs.

"What are you doing in there?" Louisa took the carton out of her hand and shooed her away. "I have everything ready to make an omelet. It will only take a few moments."

Abby decided not to argue with Louisa about her domain. "Thanks."

"Well, you must be all right if you're hungry," Dolores teased. "Sleeping late agrees with you. You look well rested."

Abby almost burned her tongue by taking a nervous gulp of coffee. She'd actually gotten less sleep than usual...because of Tripp.

"Why don't you sit outside," Louisa suggested. "It's a fine day. I'll bring the food out when it's ready."

Grateful for the change of subject, Abby smiled at the cook and moved toward the door.

As Dolores slid into a chair opposite her on the veranda, she drew in a deep breath and gazed out at the ocean. The thwack of a tennis ball and a man's triumphant shout drifted from the direction of the tennis court. "What a gorgeous morning. I thought that storm last night was one of the hurricanes we talked about at dinner. But now here it is, all clear and beautiful again as if nothing happened. This place is amazing."

The squall had been like a hurricane to Abby. Before the storm, Tripp had told her that he didn't want her, that what had transpired at the pool had been a mistake. But the wind, the rain, the lightning had destroyed some invisible barrier between the two of them and the truth shone through. She couldn't pretend that nothing had happened. Tripp wanted her, and she knew it. And she undeniably wanted him.

Abby couldn't prevent a satisfied grin. "This place *is* amazing," she said, although her thoughts were on Tripp rather than Leah's Cay.

"Well, it certainly looks as though it has healed you."

"What do you mean?" Abby cocked her head.

"The last time I was here you were all business. As if this place would whither without your complete attention." Dolores's smile looked wistful. "Now you're sleeping late and looking...satisfied. I'm glad you've found some peace."

Abby felt a slight jab of guilt and didn't know quite what to say. She knew Dolores was the one searching for peace. Her husband had died a year ago and she still seemed to be paralyzed, unsure of how to go on without him. "It looks like *you're* doing better now," she said cautiously. "Have you made any decisions?"

Dolores sighed. "Not really. I am better. Coming here with Shannon helps. But when Shannon goes back to school, I'll be alone again. There are so many things I could do—travel, get another degree, go back out into the business world. But I can't seem to get started. And our house is so empty...."

"Well, you know you're always welcome here," Abby said, and meant it. "If you're happy on Leah's Cay, then come here as often as you like."

Louisa arrived with a tray of food for Abby and fresh coffee for Dolores. Abby wished she could do more to help. She remembered how devastated she'd been when Leah had been killed in a car accident. She'd been able to share her grief with Leah's father, then two years later he had died.

It suddenly struck her that for the first time in a long time, she didn't feel alone anymore. Because of Tripp. For the last two years, since she'd let Larry go, and turned Leah's Cay into a resort, she'd been quietly going about the business of being a gracious hostess, putting her own life aside. Now she felt like making some noise.

"Well, I think we need to liven things up around here," Abby stated. "Why don't we plan a party? We could put together a barbecue or a luau. Something fun with music, food—the works. What do you think?"

THINKING WOULD RUIN everything. So, Tripp decided against it. He pushed the Donzi to a faster speed and the roar of the engine edged out the headache that had been building behind his eyes. The wind buffeted his chest with enough power to send him tumbling backward if he hadn't been braced against the padded seat. He should be hungover, but he only had a slight headache. He should be packing his stuff and running as fast as he could, away from Leah's Cay. Away from Abby. But he was headed back there now. He should be feeling like a total heel for breaking his word.

But he felt terrific.

Last night with Abby had settled everything inside him. Not that he knew where they were headed, he just knew that the attraction, the "thing" between them was right. He didn't have to worry about her and Rick. She didn't want Rick, she wanted Tripp...physically, anyway. And that was enough to make him feel like laughing and flying low in a boat after half a bottle of tequila and three hours' sleep.

He couldn't leave now. He had to play it out, take whatever she wanted to give. Right or wrong, whether he got his boat back or not, she would have to tell him to go when the time came. And he refused to speculate on when that time would be. He just knew he couldn't leave. Not now.

He throttled the boat back as Leah's Cay came into sight. He wondered if she was up yet. She hadn't been earlier when he'd slipped in through the kitchen door for his usual coffee. He and the girls had set the pelican free after naming him Toby. Then because he had way too much nervous energy running through him, he'd gone back to the mangroves near the dock and cut down every piece of fishing line that could accidentally snag another bird.

He wished he could have slept late with Abby. Of course if he had, they might still be in bed like those newlyweds in the main suite.

A glimmer of unease ran through his good mood. He and Abby would never have that luxury. He didn't have the right to lie around in bed with her. As a matter of fact, he'd pretty much abandoned the sinking ship of his honor last night in the storm. And clung to Abby like a drowning man.

He cut the engine. As the boat glided to the dock, he decided he had absolutely no sane reason to be happy. But the anticipation of seeing Abby this morning after loving her so thoroughly last night wouldn't go away. He couldn't stop smiling as he tied the boat.

10

AFTER SECURING THE BOAT, Tripp casually checked the mansion via the kitchen. No Abby. He crossed the grounds and checked the pool. He found her there, swimming laps. And he watched her, as he'd done so many other mornings. Standing in the breezeless heat of the trees, he tortured himself by following every move she made as she left the water and patted her skin dry with a towel.

Each memory of the taste of her, the feel of her the night before, sizzled through him like heat lightning, and he'd wanted her again. The fantasy was real now and stronger than he'd expected. Very close to being more than he could resist. But he had no choice. The two teenagers were camped on chaises at the opposite side of the pool, reading books and sunbathing. When Abby smiled at some comment Shannon made that he couldn't hear, the dull thud of his tequila-induced headache returned.

"Get a grip," he said under his breath as he adjusted the hard evidence of his arousal. He needed to move, to get out of there before his good mood was totally wrecked. With his luck, Rick would show up next. A fast, four-mile run would sweat out the last effects of the tequila. It would also distract his thoughts from Abby until he could pull her into his arms without an audience. Concentrating on that mission, he turned away from his view of the pool, stepped out of the trees and bumped right into Dolores—Mrs. Delgado—on the walkway.

"Uh—sorry," he managed to say.

Caught by surprise, she didn't speak immediately. She looked him up and down, from his sweaty, clinging T-shirt to his cutoffs, which had suddenly become too tight. Then as he watched, the surprise faded, replaced by a narrowed look of speculation. That made Tripp uneasy. If she asked, he had no idea how to explain what he'd been doing.

"Good morning," she said finally. Not asking, but making the greeting sound like a question.

Instead of offering excuses, he smiled. *Caught in the act*, he thought in disgust. He'd been so mesmerized by Abby, he'd been oblivious to anything else. It was a good thing Carlos hadn't hired him as a lifeguard. There would be dozens of floating bodies in the pool— all except Abby's.

"Morning." Then he walked away, leaving Dolores to her own conclusions.

"MOM? TRIPP SAYS we need to leave for the sandbar in the next half hour. The tide is changing," Shannon said. Sitting on the veranda again for lunch, surrounded by Dolores, Rick and the other two lawyers, Abby could see Tripp down at the dock preparing the Donzi. She'd yet to speak to him this morning, but after last night she wasn't worried. Last evening had been a roller coaster ride of emotions, but after spending the night in his arms she finally felt steady, on solid ground. She knew they would be together again, alone, and she could wait. She had only to get through Tuesday evening with Carlos and Rick first.

"Abby?" Dolores interrupted her thoughts. "What exactly goes on at this sandbar?"

Dolores actually looked worried, and that surprised Abby. "It's a movable party. When the tide goes out, the water in the flats gets very shallow, forming sort of a beach. Boats anchor along the channel so people can sunbathe, listen to music and socialize. There's even a couple of boats that sell drinks." She smiled at Shannon and Kayla who were outfitted in their new bathing suits and ready to go. "There are lots of *guys* there."

"Come on, Mom. Put on your bathing suit. Let's go," Shannon pleaded.

"All right." Dolores gave in but turned to Abby. "Come with us."

Dolores seemed so uncertain that Abby gave in without a fight. After their talk this morning, she knew Dolores needed to get out, even if it merely meant an afternoon watching tanned and oiled bodies cruise by. And the thought of spending a few hours in close proximity to Tripp would be icing on the cake.

"Let's go get changed," Abby said.

After excusing themselves and entering the house,

Dolores stopped Abby before she could head upstairs to her room.

"Abby?" Dolores looked around before stepping closer to speak. "What do you know about Tripp?"

Abby was so surprised by the question, she laughed. It was exactly what she'd asked Louisa several days ago. "What do you mean?"

"I mean... Is he...okay?"

As far as Abby was concerned, Tripp was way past "okay." But since Dolores looked so serious, she kept the comment to herself. "Yes. Why do you ask?"

"Well...you see, this morning, on the way to the pool, I bumped into him."

Abby remembered when Dolores had come out to bring the girls more sunblock, but Abby couldn't fathom where this conversation was going. "And?" she prodded.

"He was— I mean it looked like he was—" Frustrated, she pushed on, "Well, *aroused*. He was standing in the trees, watching the girls at the pool."

"Watching the girls?"

"And you. He stepped out of the trees and didn't see me. You had just finished your laps when I got there."

"What did he say?"

"Nothing. Oh, he said good morning and he smiled. That was it." She looked uncomfortable. "That's why I wanted you to go with us today."

Abby laughed, unconcerned. She remembered standing in the trees, watching *him* swim. After last night, she doubted he'd been ogling the girls, but made a mental note to call him on it. "I wouldn't worry." She squeezed Dolores's hand. "I can vouch for him." That was one way to put it. She could vouch *for* him, with him, under him and on top of him. They'd already proven that. She wished she could tell everyone, but she remembered what Tripp had said about complications. She knew he was right. Talking about what was happening between them would be a mistake. "He's okay," she added.

STANDING ABOARD the Donzi, Tripp watched Rick approach, along with Shannon and Kayla, and wondered what was up. He continued setting out seat cushions and stowing gear until they were close enough to speak.

"Hey, Tripp," Rick called. "You mind if I tag along? The girls invited me."

Tripp looked at the two teenagers, barely covered by skimpy bikinis, then back to Rick. There would be enough adolescent hormones at the sandbar to send the girls into overload. And enough bikinis on the over-twenty-one set for Rick to enjoy. It would give the lawyer something to think about besides Abby, and since she wasn't going with them...

"Sure," he answered, feeling magnanimous. "You can help me fend off the beach bums."

The girls made a show of whining. "No fair."

Tripp laughed. Then he saw Abby in a bathing suit, walking toward the dock with Dolores, and his mood deflated. The initial pleasure at realizing she intended to go along was scuttled by the fact that Rick would be there, too. Wasn't it enough that Rick would have her all to himself on the long drive to Miami for dinner? But then, the last few days with her hadn't been enough for Tripp. Each time he touched her only seemed to increase his need to touch her again. He lowered his chin and leveled a hard look at the lawyer, thinking he could warn him off somehow, but Rick had turned to watch Abby approach.

Tripp's earlier pleasant mood changed. Instead of being able to put aside reality and spend time with Abby, he was forcibly reminded that he only worked at the resort. It was his job to drive the boat for the guests...for Abby. He tightened his jaw and walked forward to start the engine.

"IT'S SO HOT." Dolores sighed, fanning herself with the magazine she'd brought along to read. Even though Tripp had rigged an awning to provide shade, the sun, unrelieved by clouds, beat down relentlessly on the assembly of boats anchored along the channel. The breeze had died and heat seemed to radiate in the air, mixed with the sound of boat engines and a variety of music blaring from different sources.

"Reminds me of Saturday night after a college football game," Abby said. Just then, two boys on a Wave Runner buzzed by them and jumped the wake of one of the passing boats. "Except with boats instead of cars."

Dolores shaded her eyes and scanned the people walking and playing Frisbee with dogs in the shallower water. "Where are the girls?"

"I'm keeping an eye on them," Tripp said. He stood

up, and stretched his spine in a lazy manner. "They're near the boat with the loudest boombox. Headed back this way."

Dolores gave Abby a meaningful look that almost made her laugh. She guessed Dolores wanted her to notice that he was watching the girls again, but any comment she could make was forestalled by Tripp's movement. In an easy motion, he skinned off his T-shirt, levered off his athletic shoes and moved to the back of the boat.

Watching him, Abby had to agree with Dolores—it *was* hot. Getting hotter by the moment. As Tripp bent to tie a line to a red rubber diver's float, she felt her temperature rise. His broad back was tanned and far too tempting. She wanted to walk up behind him and put her arms around his waist. It suddenly seemed like a long time since she'd touched him.

Rick's voice interrupted her thoughts. "This is better than Spring Break," he said, sounding amazed.

Abby glanced at him and then in the direction he was looking. Five women in bikinis were dancing to the sounds of Gloria Estefan and waving to people from the deck of a large cabin cruiser named *The Other Woman* as it passed by them in the channel. As the wake of the big boat rocked the Donzi, Tripp tossed the float he'd secured into the current, stepped up on the step and dove over the side into the water.

Rick dug through the cooler Tripp had loaded into the boat. "Want a soda or a beer?" he asked.

Restless and wanting to abandon ship along with

Tripp, Abby stood and made an effort to choose among the drinks in the cooler. She decided on bottled water. Beer would only make her hotter and the situation more frustrating. She looked over the side and saw Tripp, eyes closed, floating on his back in the current, one arm hooked around the float. He looked totally at ease. Unlike her, he seemed to be content to enjoy the afternoon without touching. She felt like dumping the bottle of cold water over her head.

Tripp needed to cool off. The heat from the sun was only part of the problem. He'd tried to ignore Abby, but he couldn't. And every time Dolores caught him staring, she frowned. She'd obviously made some assumption about him after bumping into him near the pool.

Watching Abby rub sunblock over her arms and legs had nearly killed him. Each time he looked at her and remembered her fevered response to him the night before, he'd wanted to swear. He'd wanted to throw caution over the side and pull her to him in front of Dolores, Rick and the whole world. He could almost feel how hot her skin would be, slicked by suntan lotion and sweat. The vision had forced him off the boat and into the water. He had to cool off and calm down.

Floating in the current, he forced his thoughts to his boat and what he'd do when he got it back. Sailing had been his passion, the center of his life, and he needed to get back to it. To his own future. The idea of sailing the islands again, free from commitments or deals, eased some of the tension inside him. *Having no plan, and sticking to it.* On his boat, he could relax and do whatever the hell he wanted. His only concern would be the wind and the ocean. And being away from Abby.

The sudden fantasy of Abby, sailing with him through the blue-green waters of the Caribbean sluiced through him. The idea of having her, alone, touching her when he wanted—when *she* wanted—was more tantalizing than any thoughts he'd ever had of heaven. Just the two of them. No resort, no watchful friends, no lawyers—

A loud splash disturbed the water near him, spraying him with drops, then a body bumped his and he heard girlish laughter. He opened his eyes. No resort, no friends, no lawyers— And as one of them grabbed his arm to stay afloat, he finished his prior list—no teenagers.

He blinked the water out of his eyes and looked up as the girls nearly pushed him under with their effort to tread water. Dolores was standing at the side of the boat, along with Rick and Abby. Rick and Abby were smiling, Dolores appeared ready to attack.

He peeled Kayla's determined hands from his arm and used the rope to pull himself into water shallow enough to stand in.

"You girls know how to play basketball?" he asked from a safe distance. When they answered in the affirmative, he turned to the boat. "Rick, open the front locker and hand me the floating hoop, will you?" A plan was taking form. He needed to get everyone in the water.

Rick leaned over the side, a can of imported beer in

one hand, holding the hoop out to him with the other. Exactly what Tripp wanted. He slid off the bottom into the deeper water, moving slightly out of reach. Rick leaned farther. He could have tossed the hoop, but thank goodness it hadn't occurred to him. Waiting for the right moment, as the wake from another boat rose beneath the Donzi, Tripp grabbed the hoop and pulled. Rick forgot to let go and tumbled into the water. He came up sputtering next to Tripp.

"Hey! You made me spill my beer!" Rick said as he reached for the rapidly sinking container. Shannon and Kayla whooped in approval as Rick poured salt water out of the can and tossed it into the boat.

"Since you're here," Tripp said, making an effort not to smile too broadly, "how about tying the hoop to the float?" Without giving Rick time to retaliate, Tripp pushed the hoop into his hands and swam to the back of the boat. "Hey, Abby, throw me the ball."

Abby was sitting on the side, shaking her head and smiling. She went to find the ball but when she returned, she gave him a fake, meaningful scowl, then called to Shannon, "Head's up!" before tossing the ball to her.

"I don't trust you," she said, grinning down at Tripp with her hands on her hips.

For just a moment, he forgot himself. He remembered the peaceful expression on her face as she'd slept in his arms. "Yes, you do," he said, and watched her eyes widen at the innuendo. He moved past it quickly, purposely not checking to see if Dolores had caught the

Night Heat

double meaning. "You two, come on in and play," he taunted, and swiveled toward Rick. "How about it, Rick? Men against the girly-girls."

"I think I'll watch," Dolores answered as Abby slid into the water.

"Three against two." Tripp shook his head in a false gesture of worry still directed at Rick. "That ought to give them a slight chance."

The game was on.

Playing basketball on a court was one thing; trying to maintain any kind of coordination in the water was impossible. By the first time-out, Abby felt half-drowned. A condition that didn't bother her too much. She knew if she really went under, Tripp would pull her back up. Every time she managed to get the ball, Tripp seemed to be there. And in the guise of guarding the basket, he took any opportunity to surreptitiously handle her. From the first jump for possession of the ball he'd stayed close to her, relegating the two teenagers to Rick.

With a score of fourteen to eight, the girls could at least hold their heads up...sort of. The guys weren't killing them too bad. They'd drawn a small audience of three teenage boys who'd gathered in the shallower water, probably in response to watching Shannon and Kayla jump up and down in their bikinis. Even Dolores laughed and applauded when the girls got a basket.

During the second half, the game got a little more serious. The females had devised a plan to feed Shannon the ball since Rick couldn't guard both of them. It worked, partially.

Abby faked a shot then tossed the ball to Shannon. Since she was closer to Tripp than Rick, Tripp had to block. Abby moved back out of the way and ended up between Rick and Kayla. Then, because Tripp intimidated Shannon, she shrieked and passed the ball back to Abby.

Abby wound up trapped by Rick. They wrestled good-naturedly for the ball, both going under in the process. They came up sputtering and laughing. Choking on saltwater, Abby called a time-out. Rick's hand was on her arm steadying her because he was taller and could touch bottom.

Abby pushed her wet hair out of her face and looked into Tripp's eyes. *Game over.* He was staring at Rick with an unreadable expression. Unreadable, but not particularly friendly. Before things got too serious, Abby tossed the ball back to Shannon—a blatant breach of rules during a time-out—and yelled, "What are you? A chicken? Shoot it!" She made a face at Tripp. "He's not as mean as he looks." They all scrambled for positions once more and the game continued.

BY THE TIME the dock of Leah's Cay came into view, Tripp had regained his good mood. He'd almost lost it when he'd seen Rick's hands on Abby and realized that tonight the lawyer would be spending an entire evening with her. It wasn't Abby's fault or even Rick's that Tripp couldn't publicly touch the woman he wanted. But privately... Now *that* was a different story. And he intended to see her privately before she left for Miami.

He glanced back over his shoulder at the passengers in the boat. Everyone appeared whipped. Sunburned and unusually still, the girls seemed content that their first trip to the sandbar had been a success. They'd ended up playing a second game of water basketball with the teenage boys who'd shown up to watch and had invited them to visit Leah's Cay.

Sometime during the afternoon, Dolores had stopped giving him unfriendly looks. He supposed that was a good sign although he didn't know what he'd done to change her mind.

Rick had his feet propped up, consoling himself with a beer, while Abby sat in the seat across from him with her head back and eyes closed. Tripp knew *she* had to be worn-out...after he'd kept her awake most of the night before. Maybe she'd be too tired to go to Miami tonight. He turned his attention back to the stretch of water between the boat and the dock in order to hide his smile.

11

ABBY DRESSED very carefully for dinner. She wanted to look sophisticated and understated in deference to Carlos Cezare's world view. Carlos had a traditional vision about the image that people, with the kind of money she'd inherited, should convey. So she'd chosen a cocktail length designer dress in basic black. But she also wanted to appear untouchable in case Rick did have an agenda. She added a single strand of pearls for class and distance.

There had only been a moment to speak to Tripp alone after the afternoon spent at the sandbar. She'd asked him to meet her near the fountain in the formal garden at four-thirty. She'd told Rick to meet her at five at the opposite end of the house.

It seemed so silly, she almost laughed. After being alone this long, she suddenly had two men to deal with. It reminded her of high school. Except these men were all grown up. She needed to act like an adult herself, yet she couldn't leave with Rick until she'd seen Tripp, not after last night. If that need was juvenile, then she'd have to plead guilty to advanced adolescence.

As she slipped through the rear door of the house into the late-afternoon warmth, she shivered. Her dress felt sleek and cool against her skin, her stockings caressed her legs like moving water...and she knew Tripp was in the garden, waiting.

A shaft of bright sunlight made the splashing water in the fountain sparkle as it tumbled over the painted tiles. The garden seemed empty. Abby slowed her steps and glanced around the well-kept area. There were lush hibiscus bushes blooming in vivid reds and yellows, carnival-striped crotons and several combinations of bougainvillea. At one end, under the shade of gumbo-limbo trees, a myriad of orchid plants hung from pieces of bark in the lower branches.

When two warm hands slid up along her arms and pulled her back against a hard body, she didn't jump or resist. She knew the touch, and a sharp spasm of exhilaration bolted through her.

Tripp kissed her lightly on the neck and murmured, "Hello." She leaned into him, drew in a deep breath and smiled, completely content now that Tripp was there. Then he turned her to face him.

Abby watched him scrutinize her from head to toe before dropping his hands away as if he might wrinkle her dress.

He seemed to choose his words with care. "You look...incredible," he said in a low, caressing tone that made her want to laugh and hug him.

"Thank you," she said, then returned the compliment. "So do you." Tripp had showered, shaved and dressed in a pair of canvas shorts and a polo shirt. He looked cool and relaxed and...kissable.

And Abby wanted to be kissed. She ran her palms up the soft cotton covering his chest and stepped closer. Wearing heels made him easier to reach.

He resisted for a second, but then, his hands were on her, pulling her to him. His mouth met hers and melded into a slow, spine-melting kiss that left her breathless.

"We smeared your lipstick," Tripp breathed when they broke apart. Abby's arms remained loosely clasped around his neck as he used his thumb to rub away the evidence on her lower lip.

"I don't care. I can fix it," Abby replied, not worried in the least. "I've missed you, even though we were together all afternoon."

"I know what you mean," he agreed, and kissed her lightly again. When she would have deepened the kiss, he pulled back. His features settled into a slight frown. "About tonight..."

Abby waited and watched Tripp take a deep breath and let it out.

"Hell," he said, and looked down for a second. "It's not that I don't want you to enjoy yourself." His gaze met hers again. "I just don't want you to *enjoy* yourself," he added with meaning. "Not with Rick."

He seemed so serious, she couldn't resist the urge to tease him. "How about you? I heard you were ogling the girls at the pool this morning."

"Ogling?" he repeated, only half-amused. "I was taking their names in vain. If they hadn't been there, you and I would have ended up in the pool again—with no swimming involved. I'm always watching you," he added, his blue gaze holding her hostage. "Haven't you felt it?"

Abby had to swallow to ease the lump in her throat. "Every time I look at you, you seem to be walking away," she said in amazement.

"Not anymore."

"Good, I'd rather have you close by. I like the way you look at me."

Tripp gazed into Abby's wide amber eyes and felt like he'd fallen out of a plane and hit the water, chest first. He could hardly breathe. He knew in that moment he loved her. Not lust, not protectiveness—love. How had that happened? How had she gotten inside him? Was it when she'd given herself to him that first night in the pool? Or was it when she slept so trustingly in his arms after he'd tried his best to keep her at a distance?

Love. He knew it was true. And he knew it would be a disaster for both of them. Because he'd have to give her up and soon.

Carlos wanted Rick to have her.

Tripp was being selfish. Rick would be better for Abby than Tripp could ever be. Rick could probably buy and sell him several times over. Abby certainly could. As he held her in his arms, dressed in her beautiful clothes he wondered what Abby wanted. In a perfect world he could offer her his love and a future together. In this world, he couldn't think of one damned thing he could offer her besides what they'd shared the night before. The one thing he knew she wanted. Hot, breathless, mind-blowing sex.

He could hold her with sex—for a little while. But ultimately that wouldn't be enough for a woman like Abby, and she shouldn't have to choose one or the other. She deserved the whole package—a lover, a partner...the truth. He couldn't even offer that much.

He was planning to leave. As soon as he got his boat back, he'd sail out of her life and into his own lifelong dream. The world awaited him—courtesy of the *Wisp*. Here in the garden, with Abby in his arms, the idea of leaving her behind suddenly seemed like more than he could manage. What if he couldn't do it? Leave without her?

Like he had a choice. When she found out he'd lied to her, she'd probably have him thrown off the estate.

But he still couldn't bow out, push her in Rick's direction as Carlos wanted. Not yet. After months of watching her, looking out for her, he wouldn't be there tonight. Just thinking about it made his hands tighten on her back, made him desperate to kiss her again.

"Remember...tonight—not with Rick," he murmured against her lips as he did his best to convince her.

Too SHORT A TIME later, Abby opened the back door to the mansion. She glanced back before stepping through. Tripp remained in the garden, near the fountain, where she'd left him. Watching her.

She hadn't wanted to leave him. In fact, she could hardly force herself to walk through the door. She wished she had the nerve to call Carlos and say she didn't feel well, that Rick would have to go alone. But when she finally, reluctantly, entered the house, she found Dolores waiting for her.

"I thought Tripp was watching the girls. He was actually watching you, wasn't he?" she asked, although she already seemed to know the answer.

Dolores had obviously seen her in the garden with Tripp. A blush of embarrassment moved up her neck before she realized that she didn't need to be embarrassed. She wasn't a teenager like Shannon, and Dolores wasn't her mother. If she wanted to kiss Tripp, her employee, she could.

Her rebellious thoughts fizzled as she stared at her friend. "I, um— We're sort of—" *What?* her mind scrambled.

"He's in love with you," Dolores said.

"What?" Abby might have laughed if she hadn't been so shocked. "No, we're...involved, I guess you could say. But love, no."

"*He's* in love. If you could see the way he looks at you..."

"He can't be. It's only—" she stared into Dolores's confident expression and faltered "—been less than a week."

"WOULD YOU LIKE something to drink?" Rick asked as he studied the different bottles in the limo's well-stocked bar.

Abby fidgeted with her beaded handbag and finally

decided a good stiff drink might help. "Yes," she answered.

"We have Chivas Regal, Tanqueray, Stolichnaya, Cristal..."

"I'll have whatever you're having," she demurred, unable to make any more choices.

"Champagne, I think," Rick said, lifting the bottle of chilled Cristal and working the wire like a man who was accustomed to drinking champagne in a limo. He handed her two crystal flutes before popping the cork and pouring them each a glass.

Abby took a healthy sip of the bubbling wine, hoping it would calm her, or cool her, or just get her silly enough not to care about leaving Tripp alone in the garden.

He's in love with you.

Dolores's words seemed to blare in her head. And even though she'd dismissed Dolores's assumption to her face...her friend hadn't faltered. *If you could see the way he looks at you.* Abby had wanted to explain that those heated looks were lust—not love. That she and Tripp had been unable to keep their hands off each other for the past few days. But Dolores had obviously made up her mind.

"How is it?" Rick asked, jarring Abby back to the present.

"Very good," she answered, and took another long sip.

Rick watched her with unnerving intentness. He seemed relaxed and willing to let her lead the conversation. Maybe he'd guessed she was nervous about being alone with him in the back of a limo for two hours.

"Have you been enjoying your vacation?" she asked in an attempt at small talk.

"Very much." He glanced out of the tinted window as they crossed over one of the many bridges between Leah's Cay and the mainland. "It's beautiful here. I could relocate from Philly and not miss the city for a minute," he added.

Rick didn't move closer, or smile, or do anything to make her uncomfortable, except to say, "I would like to spend a little more time getting to know you, though."

"Really?" Abby sipped the last of the champagne in her glass and held the flute out for Rick to refill. She had no idea what Rick's idea of "getting to know her" meant. "Well, you've seen the normal operation of the resort. Making sure the guests are comfortable and enjoying themselves takes up most of my time. There isn't a whole lot more to tell."

He smiled indulgently. Instead of trying to corner her, as she'd expected, Rick relaxed back in the seat, giving her plenty of room. "What do you think of capital punishment?" he asked.

Before she could come up with an answer to such an off-the-wall question, he asked another. "Who would you rather meet? Howard Stern or Rush Limbaugh?"

By the time the limo rolled over the Card Sound Bridge forty-five minutes later Abby was laughing. The champagne helped, but Rick had an acerbic wit for such a straight-looking guy. She decided that one evening with him wouldn't be a total hardship.

Even Grumpy Cezare surprised her by being in excellent spirits. He welcomed Rick into his stately Bayshore Drive home like they were old friends, although he insisted on calling him Richard. Virginia, Carlos's wife, fussed over Rick and Abby as if they were part of her extended family.

Dinner was excellent—a mix of the old standbys with the new: roast pork with guava chutney, black beans and rice topped with chopped red Bermuda onions, fried plantains glazed with lime and honey, and homemade mango ice cream with sugar wafers. Abby spent her time eating and listening to Carlos and *Richard* discuss everything from the weather to the stock market. She felt so full, she could hardly move by the end of the evening.

That's when Carlos asked to speak with her privately in his office. They excused themselves from Rick and Virginia for a few moments.

"Here are the papers I would like you to sign," Carlos said, setting a folder in front of her. As she opened the folder and uncapped the pen next to it, he walked around to the business side of his desk, sat across from her and steepled his hands on the smooth mahogany surface.

Abby briefly scanned the papers then signed them without questions. She trusted Carlos implicitly. Leah's father had been his close friend, and Abby knew that a man like Carlos would never dishonor a friendship. After she signed and closed the folder she looked up.

Carlos scrutinized her for what seemed like an inordinately long time. Long enough to cause Abby to shift in her chair. She wondered if her hair had done something funky, or if part of her dinner was decorating the front of her dress. Transforming her personal image from normal to "elegant" with the help of unlimited funds had taken time and work. Carlos had taught her that when you have enough to buy anything, you should only buy the best. She winced slightly. Sometimes even buying the best didn't equate with wearing an image well.

"Is there something else?" she asked, refusing to look down to check her dress.

Carlos lowered his hands and held her with his gaze. "There is something I would ask you to do," he said.

"Certainly." She'd always followed Carlos's advice, even when it had been painful. Like when he'd advised her not to marry Larry and backed the advice up with hard, cold facts. "What is it?" she ventured.

"I would like you to hear a proposal. To do so, with an open mind."

"A proposal? What kind of proposal?" Abby asked in relief, picturing another trip to Miami to meet with his investment group or to see a piece of property.

Carlos stared at her again, as if to measure how much to tell her, and Abby's consternation reappeared. He'd never been secretive before. Finally he spoke.

"I am aware that we are from different generations,

different cultures. But I ask you to consider what you will hear with the knowledge that I only want the best for you. I know George Axillar would want me to treat you the same as his daughter, or my own, in this matter."

This matter. Abby was so perplexed, she didn't speak. Carlos stood then, stepped around the desk and offered her his arm.

"Come with me."

A picture flashed through her mind of Grumpy walking her down the aisle, giving her away at her wedding. She smiled slightly at her fancifulness. Carlos handled her business, but she realized that if she ever did marry, she'd want him there. She had no one left to do the honors.

When they returned to the living room, where they'd left Rick and Virginia, the room was empty. Carlos didn't appear surprised by this and unerringly guided her past the leather couches, over the marble floors cushioned by plush Oriental rugs to a set of doors that opened onto a tiled portico. He stopped and held the door open for Abby, but instead of following her through, he closed it behind her.

The view was spectacular, lights from the homes and businesses around Biscayne Bay twinkled in the distance framed by two huge ficus trees. A breeze carrying the scent of jasmine stirred the white blooms of bougainvillea spilling over the railing.

Rick, who'd obviously been enjoying the view, turned at the sound of the door closing. He shoved his hands in his pockets, betraying the same nervousness he'd shown when he'd asked her out at the resort.

Suddenly Abby put Carlos's two and two together—proposal and daughter. The shock of coming up with four and the serious expression on Rick's face held her motionless.

"Abby?" Rick said.

ABBY! Tripp's mind seemed to resonate with the sound. After watching Rick settle her in the back of the limo for their ride to Miami, Tripp had escaped from the resort, hoping to outrun thoughts of what might be happening between them. He'd spent most of the evening with Jimmy Rittner, drinking beer and demolishing several baskets of boiled shrimp in the process, finding out that Jimmy had about as much business sense as a ten-pound grouper.

After hearing some of the facts and figures involving Jimmy's *Miss Behavin'*, Tripp could only shake his head. The man should never have gone into the charter business for himself. The direness of Jimmy's situation, in some ways mirroring his own legal disasters, had almost taken his mind off Abby and Rick.

Almost.

Now, as he turned down the gravel road toward Leah's Cay, the scene of his fall from grace, the setting for his fall into "love," which equaled emotional Russian roulette, and the sum total of his last God-given chance, Tripp felt beat. He'd never thought of himself as a loser, but the longer he fought reality, the harder and faster life seemed to line up to prove him wrong.

He'd end up a loser like hard-drinking, good-natured, total screwup Rittner. In Tripp's opinion, Jimmy didn't have a chance to save his boat—not unless someone came along with a truckload of money and bought the liens back for him.

Tripp could see his own story written on the same wall. His last chance had been blown to hell by his weakness, by falling for the one woman he was supposed to protect. There was no one to blame but himself. The future looked like a hurricane on the horizon, and he couldn't stop the rain, or the lightning, or the wind. He could have Abby for a very short period of time, or have his boat if Carlos never found out that he'd broken his word. But chances were that everything was finished for him. Carlos wanted Rick to court Abby.

And he'd promised to speak to Carlos for Jimmy.

Tripp pulled into the drive behind the main house and parked his Jeep. It was only ten-thirty, too early for him to start worrying. He figured the earliest Abby could get back would be midnight. He glanced up at her balcony as he walked past, then headed for the pool to swim laps and clear his head.

"WOULD YOU LIKE to sit down?" Rick asked, indicating a cushioned white chair near a small table.

"No thanks," Abby replied. "I've been sitting all

night." She looked past him to the view. "This is really beautiful."

"Yes, it is," he agreed, without turning to admire the lights reflecting on the water. "Are you sure you wouldn't like to sit?"

He wanted her to sit down—that much was clear. "All right." She complied, sitting on the edge of the chair.

Rick pulled another chair closer and sat near enough for their knees to brush. He drew in a deep breath, then exhaled. "Abby, I..."

Gone was the charm and the acerbic wit of earlier in the evening. He seemed so uncomfortable, she wished she could help him, although she wasn't sure she wanted to hear what he intended to say. "Yes?"

"I don't know how to do this, other than to just say it. So, here goes...." He held her gaze. "I know who you are."

"Excuse me?"

He barreled onward. "I know that you've been keeping a secret, that you own Leah's Cay and several—"

"What?" Abby felt like she was falling. The very ground beneath her seemed to shift—not in space, but time, as if she'd stepped back two years and had to face Larry all over again. "Why? How did you—?"

"Please, hear me out, okay?" Rick reached over and took her hand in his.

Abby didn't resist. She needed something to hold on to just then. His hand was warm, which meant that hers must be ice-cold.

"Mr. Cezare and I have talked and—"

"Carlos told you about me?" She hadn't intended to interrupt again but she couldn't quite get it straight in her mind. Larry's image and memory had overlapped Rick somehow.

Rick let out a breath and leaned back; he kept possession of her hand. "Yes. We've talked, and he feels that you and I might have a lot in common."

Determined not to stop him again, Abby nodded.

Rick seemed to take that as a good sign and relaxed slightly. "Look, I want to be completely honest with you. I know you had a bad experience in the past. I've gone through something similar.

"Remember when I told you that I was unattached and would like to get to know you?"

"Yes," Abby replied.

"I meant it. But the rest of that statement is, I don't want your money. I have plenty of my own. My family name is Herrington, of the Philadelphia Herringtons."

Abby knew he was telling her the truth. Carlos would have never gone to such lengths to introduce them—in his own home—without checking Rick's financial standing. Not after Larry.

"So Carlos is matchmaking?" Abby said, not knowing if she should hug Grumpy or kill him.

"You could say that. We met at a law convention and he asked if I'd ever been to the Florida Keys. That perhaps I should consider a vacation."

Abby could almost hear Carlos speaking those words.

Rick leaned his elbows on his knees and leaned toward her. The warm light from the interior of the house beyond the doors lit his face. He looked sincere and as earnest as a high school senior on Prom Night. *I'll have her home by midnight, Mr. Cezare.* She wondered what kind of woman had hurt him by trying to marry into his money. *The same kind of person as Larry.*

"Here's the deal," he said, moving in for the closing argument. "I'm attracted to you, and I like you as a person. I think we'd make a good couple." He smiled and shrugged as if he knew how dopey that sounded. Abby found herself smiling back. "And I promise you two things. One, I'll always tell you the truth. Two, I'm not in it for the money." He smiled sheepishly. "I'm sorry. Doesn't sound very romantic, does it?"

"Well, no, but I gave up on romance a long time ago," Abby said, remembering Larry once more. The breeze picked up just then, rustling the foliage around them. She breathed in the exotic smell of jasmine, and for a heartbeat the memory of leaving Tripp in the garden at Leah's Cay filled her mind. Dolores's words came back to haunt her. *He's in love with you.* In the face of Rick's declaration, she needed to decide what she wanted from Tripp. She forced herself back to Rick and the present. "I don't know, Rick. I—"

He held up a hand to stop her. "Don't make any decisions tonight. I want you to think about it, though. Consider getting to know me—getting to know each other. And I want to be clear. I'm not playing a game. My ultimate goal is to get married and have a couple of kids. If you want to invest some time to see if we might try for the same goal, then tell me before I leave."

He tightened his grip on her fingers briefly before releasing them. "I can always extend my vacation."

TRIPP SAW THE LIMO pull in and glanced at his watch—12:38. In the past two hours he'd swum laps, showered, dressed, paced and finally forced himself to sit and wait. The fight for his boat had given him a few gray hairs but this thing with Abby might kill him.

The limo driver opened the door, illuminating the interior of the car. Rick stepped out, then helped Abby. She was smiling at him as they walked to the front door of the mansion.

The setting and the casting seemed perfect, like a scene from a romantic movie. The chasm between Abby's life and his own had never felt so deep or wide, and now there was a shark named Rick swimming around in it.

But Tripp still watched her—as he'd always watched her. She was back on Leah's Cay, which meant she was his business again. Except that business was the last thing on his mind. He'd never felt so unprofessional in his life.

The front door closed behind them and Tripp ran a hand over his face. Now what? Out of sight but definitely not out of mind.

ABBY DIDN'T FLINCH when Rick kissed her lightly on the cheek and said good-night. Being close to him hadn't been unpleasant. He'd charmed her in spite of herself. For the entire evening he'd been a perfect gentleman who would probably make a decent husband and father. And he'd told her the truth. Something Abby had thought she'd lost a chance at forever by becoming rich.

Upstairs, she closed the door to her room and dropped her purse on the bed. The bed. She ran her hand over the duvet and remembered—she and Tripp, naked, tangled together for one long stormy night. She hadn't thought of him in terms of a husband, a father. He didn't seem the type.

Did he love her? Or was Dolores's imagination working overtime.

She knew Tripp wanted her. And he didn't know she was rich. Rick wanted her, and he did. The opportunity to be "normal" was staring her in the face. Rick was offering her the chance to have a husband and family safely, without worrying about being fooled again. Tripp remained a stranger in her bed. She had no idea what she could expect from him in the future. What should she do?

Abby kicked off her heels and walked to the balcony doors. She twisted the handles, swung them outward and leaned on the railing that overlooked the walkway. *Tripp.* She imagined his face, his hands holding her, mapping her skin, his mouth, giving her pleasure. There was nothing ordinary about the heat between the two of them.

As if her thoughts had drawn him, like a siren song,

Tripp stepped out of the trees onto the walkway below. They stared at each other in silence for several seconds.

Then Tripp held up a hand to her as if she could fly if she wanted. "Come down."

A shock of power like a spark ran through her. She forgot about Rick and making decisions. Whatever the source of the magic between her and Tripp, it had taken hold again. Slowly, holding his gaze she reached behind her back and pulled the zipper of her dress down. The soft, slippery material fell away from her shoulders and slithered to an expensive pile at her feet.

With a knowing smile as ancient as Eve, she shook her head to his request.

"You come up."

12

"YOU MUST SPEND HALF your life in boats," Abby said as Tripp put an arm around her and pulled her close to his side.

The ocean was nearly waveless, the sun a hot yellow disc, low, rising out of the water. They'd sneaked out of the house as the first streaks of dawn lit the sky. Now they were in the Donzi, on the way to breakfast at a place called the Boatside. According to Tripp, the restaurant catered to fishermen, not tourists, serving breakfast from 6:00 a.m. to 10:00 a.m. You could park your boat practically next to your table and buy your bait on the way out.

"I wish I did spend all my time on a boat. I love being on the water," Tripp replied.

Love. Abby looked up at him, trying to read the thoughts behind those mirrored glasses. She wanted to ask what else he'd loved. Had there been a woman? If they'd been friends before becoming lovers she would have known more about him. Again she remembered Dolores's words—*He's in love with you.*

After last night she could almost believe it. The gentleness of his touch, the fact that he'd stayed, waited for her to wake up. Then he'd coaxed her into this breakfast adventure as if he couldn't stand the thought of letting her go.

At this moment, cutting through the water with his arm around her, with the wind blowing back her hair, she could briefly imagine them together, for longer than a night or a breakfast. Paradise suddenly took on a new meaning.

She wondered what, if anything, Tripp had envisioned for them in the future. Or for himself, for that matter. Did he plan to continue working at the resort? Did he think things would simply go on as they were? Abby knew there was little chance of keeping their involvement a secret for much longer. Dolores had already figured it out. What would happen when everyone knew?

He'd warned her that first night in the pool that this was a bad idea. So where did that leave them? After Rick's on-the-table declaration last night, she had to ask. She had to know.

The Boatside was already busy, half of its docking slips filled with early risers, boats bristling with fishing poles, nets and gaffs, or neat rows of air tanks held by webbed straps.

Tripp expertly maneuvered the Donzi into a space and secured it. Then he offered Abby his hand and held hers as they walked into the restaurant.

They were settled in a booth overlooking the water, finishing their breakfast before she got up the nerve to ask him what she really wanted to know. They'd talked about boats, fishermen, about the cook who seemed to make each dish he served a personal statement—everything but themselves. She decided to start with something personal but not *personal*.

"Tell me about your boat," she asked.

"My boat?"

Tripp's breakfast seemed to take a roll in his stomach. He really didn't want to talk about himself—or the *Wisp*.

"The other night, Jimmy Rittner said something about you getting your boat back."

"Oh, right. I um—I've had a few legal problems of my own. My boat is being held hostage."

He tried to make it funny, brush it off. But he was running out of ways to deflect her.

"Did it have to do with a woman? A wife?"

Tripp actually laughed before he could stop himself, but the sound was bitter. He looked away, feeling the past like a heavy hand on his ankle, dragging him under.

"As a matter of fact, it did. Not mine, however. I had a business partner. It's *his* divorce. I just got caught in the middle, or more exactly, the *Wisp* got caught in the middle." He shrugged. "But, it's a long story and pretty boring." *That ought to satisfy her*, he thought.

"What kind of boat is it?"

He'd thought wrong. She seemed determined to know everything. The shame of it was he wanted to tell her. He was proud of his boat, even if he couldn't be proud of what he was doing to keep it. "It's a forty-foot sou'wester yawl named *Wisp*, as in will o' the..."

Abby looked surprised, like she'd expected something smaller, more in line with the Donzi. As Tripp described in loving detail the teak decks, custom butterfly hatch and distinctive hull, he watched the expression on her face.

"And what will you do when you get it back?"

He noticed she didn't say if or how. As if the prospect of losing something that important to him wasn't conceivable.

He hesitated, gazing into honey brown eyes that sparkled with interest in his boat, in him. He wasn't sure how she'd take his answer, but at least he could tell her this much of the truth.

"I've always wanted to sail around the world."

There, he'd said it. Now what? Tripp had managed to dodge the worst of the bullets about his boat. The one about needing to use Abby so Carlos would get it back for him. He'd lied about why he was working at the resort, he'd lied when he let her believe he didn't know she owned Leah's Cay, but he hadn't been able to lie about what he wanted. Unfortunately, he didn't know how to add the other part. The part about wanting Abby to go with him.

He would love to show her some of the most beautiful places in the Caribbean, like Cooper Island and Gorda Sound. Deep, crystal-clear water where sea turtles and tropical fish glide under the keel as if they were in a huge private aquarium. He wanted to make love to her miles from nowhere under a sky so blue, it was impossible to tell ocean from heaven. Then he wanted to explore the waters of the world with Abby beside him.

He watched her take in the information and saw her withdraw slightly, as if he'd said he was leaving in the morning. He needed to say something.

"I—"

"Maybe I could help you get the *Wisp* back," she offered. "You know...working at the resort, I've met a lot of wealthy people. One of them might be able to loan—"

"No. I— It's being handled." *By Carlos.* He couldn't stand this. Here she was offering to help him when she'd been helping him all along without knowing it. They'd both become prisoners of their lies. *Tell her the truth,* his conscience ordered, but his heart wanted one more hour, one more day. Whatever he could have with Abby.

"I'd like to take you sailing on it someday," he said. It was the best he could do. Too late to say, *Oh, by the way, I know you own the resort and you're not very good at choosing the right men. So I'm supposed to be your bodyguard just long enough to get my boat back.*

Her expression softened slightly. "I'd like that, too," she said.

Well, there wasn't much more to be said. He couldn't make any promises. He might never recover the *Wisp*, especially now that he'd betrayed Carlos's trust and his professional relationship with Abby. He was supposed to be protecting her from unscrupulous guys like himself. Suddenly Rick came to mind.

"So how was your evening with Rick?" he asked. He tried to sound offhand but didn't succeed very well. He'd been too busy loving her to bring it up the night before, but now he wanted to hear everything.

Abby pushed her plate away and tangled her fingers together in front of her before she answered.

"He's nice," she replied.

"Nice?" *That's it?* he wanted to add. He studied her face. She looked like a poker player determined not to give away her hand. "What do you mean, 'nice'?"

"I mean, he was a gentleman. We had a pleasant dinner with Mr. Cezare and we came home. *Nice.*"

Tripp knew he was frowning. He could feel the tightness in his jaw, but he tried to fight it. "That's it?"

He watched her watch him. She blinked twice then swallowed. Every nerve ending inside him went on alert. *That wasn't it.*

"He's leaving on Sunday," she said, as if that statement answered his question.

Her reply shouted *Evasion.* But what could he say? He had no right to even ask. And, just maybe, he didn't really want to hear the answer. He stared at her, wishing things were different. Wishing...

"When will you be leaving?" she asked.

"Me?"

"Yes. When do you think you'll get the *Wisp* back?"

Tripp shrugged, feeling even more trapped. She was matter-of-factly asking his plans as if it didn't concern her one way or another.

"I haven't made any plans," he answered lamely. *What the hell could he say?*

The waitress showed up to clear the dishes, and Tripp used the interruption to bail out of the conversation. He reached across the table and took Abby's hand.

"Come on, let's get out of here."

"I KNOW IT'S NONE of my business," Dolores began, and Abby braced herself for what would come next. "But I'm a mother, and mothers worry about everything."

They sat facing each other in leather chairs next to the large windows in Abby's office. A position overlooking the view of the fountain in the garden where Dolores had seen her kiss Tripp the afternoon before.

This morning Dolores had been sitting on the veranda when Tripp and Abby returned from their early breakfast.

Abby smiled at her friend. "I bet you worried about everything even before you became a mother," she said.

Dolores relaxed and shrugged. "Let's say I worried about different things before Shannon was born. Now I tend to be mother-specific. I worry about her health, her future...her heart."

"Well, Shannon seems to be doing fine in all those departments," Abby said. "You've done a great job with her."

"Thanks. But I want to talk about you," Dolores persisted. "I'm only a guest here, I understand that. I've known you so long though, I feel connected to you. I wouldn't want you to feel alone, like there's no one to talk to. You've certainly helped *me* since Tomas died."

Abby knew Dolores was sincere, and Abby needed someone to talk to. She just couldn't find the words to confide in her. She'd grown used to keeping her own secrets. She'd stopped confiding when her best friend, Leah, had died.

How could she explain the situation between her and Tripp to Dolores when she didn't understand it herself? On the surface it looked like a simple fling, but Abby knew there was more to it than that. She just hadn't figured out what yet.

Last night he'd been silent, serious and restless, as if he thought she might disappear before he could touch her everywhere. This morning he'd been almost possessive. Jealous, although she didn't see why. She may have spent the evening with Rick, but Tripp was the one she'd invited to her bed.

And she hadn't told Tripp about Rick's proposal. There hadn't been time last night. From the first moment he'd touched her, the encounter was heated and intense. Afterward, lying naked in his arms, she couldn't bring herself to spoil the moment. *Oh, by the way, Rick wants to marry me and have a few kids. What do you think I should do?*

This morning she'd simply chickened out. She'd been hoping—and still was—for some brilliant insight, a clear dividing line between what she wanted versus the choices around her. But the situation seemed to get muddier by the moment. Now she knew that Tripp planned to leave when he got his boat back. The prospect of losing him at some unknown future date was something she definitely didn't want to discuss. Abby stared at her friend, unable to find the beginning of the story, much less the punch line. But she didn't want Dolores to think she didn't appreciate the offer.

"I'll make you a deal," she said. "When I figure out what's going on, I'll let you know."

Dolores pursed her lips, but held her peace. An awkward silence fell between them. Abby let it spin out until she couldn't take it anymore.

"I tell you what I *would* like to do," she said. "I'd like to plan that party we talked about for Saturday night. We have the sunset sail tonight, and most of the guests will be leaving on Sunday." She hesitated. Rick had asked for her answer by then. Abby didn't want to think that far in advance. Saturday night came first. "I'd like to do something fun. Maybe we can even coax the newlyweds out of their room for more than a meal."

Dolores's expression lightened somewhat, and Abby jumped at the opening to change the course of the conversation. She set down her coffee cup, walked to her desk for a legal pad and pen and returned to her chair.

"I think we need to have a band," she said, jotting down a few notes. "Maybe steel drum if we can find one on short notice. What do you think?"

BY LUNCHTIME, they had most of the party plans underway. Louisa and Dolores were busy planning a menu that included an outdoors barbecue of shrimp, steak, and ribs. Through an agency in Miami, Abby had found a steel drum band available for Saturday. In a weak moment, she'd even called and invited Carlos Cezare and his wife.

"Interesting news," Louisa said when Abby walked into the kitchen after making her calls.

"About the party?"

"No." Louisa sent an amused glance toward Dolores. "Julia says she mentioned the sailboat trip for this afternoon to the newlyweds when she took their lunch up. They would like to go along."

"Really?" Abby couldn't believe it. She slid onto a stool at the counter and smiled. "I'm not sure I'll recognize them. I haven't seen them for days."

"Ah, young love…" Louisa smiled and shook her head.

"If they don't slow down, they're liable to be old before their time," Dolores added.

"So speaks a mother," Abby teased and laughed when Dolores blushed.

TRIPP WATCHED JASON, the mate who usually worked for Jimmy, tie off the main sail, then gazed out at the deep blue water beyond the bow. They were tacking into the wind twenty miles offshore, and Tripp finally felt at home. He could breathe out here, away from the resort, away from all his legal woes in Miami.

A woman at a party had once asked him whether he didn't get lonely out on the ocean with nothing but water and wind for company. At the time he'd given her some pat answer, knowing she wasn't the type to understand the difference between solitude and loneliness. If asked now, however, his answer would be different. The only thing about land he would miss when he left would be Abby.

His gaze brushed over the back of her head. She was sitting at the bow with Dolores, Shannon, Kayla and Rick, laughing as the spray from the waves blew back in their faces. Charlie and Ray were below, playing cards. Charlie still didn't feel up to watching the sway of the waves on the horizon, even though Abby had provided him with a Dramamine patch against seasickness.

The newlyweds, snuggled together under a small canvas tarp, were enough to give Tripp a headache. They were obviously very much in love...and in lust. Tripp could almost feel the heat of their hormones a good ten feet away. He couldn't remember ever being that young, and he certainly couldn't remember being that much in love. Until now, maybe.

He shifted his gaze to Abby again and caught her looking at him. He smiled. She waved, then pulled herself up using the cabin-top handhold and began moving aft.

"Stay low and hold on," he called to her. He'd instructed the passengers about the lifelines that ran the entire length of the boat, and she wore a personal flotation device. But if the wind shifted or they hit a sizable trough, they still could get some practice at the man-overboard drill—woman in this case.

She made it back to the cockpit without mishap and dropped down onto the bench near the wheel.

"Whew! That's like walking across a bridge that's flying through the air," she said, smiling.

"Exhilarating, huh?"

"Yeah, if you like heart palpitations." To emphasize her words she pressed one hand to the middle of her chest.

Tripp had never envied five fingers quite so much.

"It's easier once you get your sea legs," he said, then forced his attention back to the sails and the water. He had to get his mind off Abby's body parts.

"So how do you like it so far?" he asked. It was a selfish question. He wanted to hear that she liked something he lived for.

"It's great, really," she said, smiling up at him. "And so quiet. That always surprises me about sailing."

"Yeah, no engine."

The snap of the sails, the "shoosh" of the bow cutting through water and the wind were the only sounds. Even surrounded by others, the cockpit felt isolated, as if they'd stolen away alone.

"Want to steer?" he asked.

"Me?" Abby looked toward Jason like he would object. Jason was busy rewinding some line and hadn't even noticed her.

"It's your boat," he said before thinking. Her gaze zeroed back on him in surprise. He couldn't retract the words and fix the blunder now; he had to go on. He shrugged, like he'd made an innocent slip of the tongue—more body parts, he thought in disgust. "I mean the resort's boat, but you're the boss. Come on, try it."

With an undecipherable look, Abby pulled herself up with the handrail. Tripp moved to one side and allowed her to step in front of him at the wheel. He still held it steady with one hand.

"What do I do?" she asked, studying the three-foot diameter of aluminum with dubious eyes.

"Put both hands on it—like in driving—ten and two."

Abby did as instructed.

"Okay, now it'll have a little pull because of the wind, so tighten your grip." Tripp let go of the wheel.

Immediately the wheel swerved left, surprising her. Their course shifted slightly and one of the sails slackened and snapped. Jason glanced in their direction as Tripp took a position behind her and put his hands over hers on the wheel. "Hold it steady," he said as he brought them back to the best tack.

Abby was in shock. Not only from the scary prospect of wrecking the boat and everyone on it, but because Tripp's hands were warm and strong, guiding hers, and his chest brushed her back with the rise of each wave beneath the bow.

The boat settled into steady progress once more, and her fear lessened. With a little practice, she could get used to this. Being caged by Tripp's strong arms was another activity she'd like to practice more often. Even as the thought of leaning back into him teased her, she noticed that Rick wasn't helping the girls search for dolphins as he had been before. He was watching her...and Tripp.

Out of habit, she made an effort to keep up appearances. "You should try this," she called to him, as if Tripp had offered a class on sailing, and she was merely one student among many.

"Hold it steady," Tripp said close to her ear, then immediately let go and stepped back. She couldn't look at him. She felt like she'd pushed him away, and being in his arms was the best thing that had happened to her all afternoon.

Rick declined a turn at the wheel, although he kept an eye on her progress. Abby steered until her arms began to ache from the constant physical tension needed to keep the boat on course. That discomfort couldn't come close to the ache in her chest from having to choose. Tripp or Rick. The choice between two worlds. She glanced over her shoulder. Tripp, his eyes hidden again behind mirrored glasses, stared beyond her, toward the horizon as if he was one man, alone on the ocean. As if he'd already disappeared out of her life.

Probably thinking about his own boat. The urge to touch him, to bring him back to the moment, to her, was overwhelming. What would she do if—when—he got the *Wisp* back and sailed away? The thought chilled her. The past week had been filled with confusion, elation and now realization. She wanted Tripp in her life.

But that would mean putting all her eggs in one basket, telling him the truth, telling everyone the truth.

How would Tripp react when he found out she owned Leah's Cay? Then, she thought of Carlos's meticulous plans for her, the effort he'd extended in finding Rick, to give her an opportunity for happiness. How would she explain Tripp to Carlos?

The whole situation was crazy and hopeless. Abby felt like crying. Instead, she gave in and called him back.

"Tripp?"

He redirected his faraway gaze to her, then stepped in to take the wheel. He didn't touch her, or smile, or say "Good job."

"Thanks," she said, and he nodded. Feeling dismissed, Abby made her way forward, past the newlyweds, back to her seat with Rick and the girls.

Shannon and Kayla spotted a pod of bottlenose dolphins and made wishes just in case the fish really could bring good luck.

Abby glanced toward Tripp and made her own wish. She wished she knew what to do.

13

"DID YOU SLEEP WELL last night?" Rick asked.

They sat on the bow of the sailboat, virtually surrounded by a breathtaking sunset. The orange-and-apricot brilliance of the sun painted the clouds with color then spilled through and blazed a fiery trail over the water. Abby had been admiring the sky, and trying to see into the future. Rick's question caught her off guard.

Such an innocuous inquiry, but she could feel heat moving up her neck into her face. She hoped the color of her blush would be attributed to the vermilion sky reflected by the sails of the boat. She'd slept, yes—with Tripp.

"Yes, I did. Very well," she answered.

"Glad to hear you didn't lose any sleep over what we discussed," he said.

Abby turned to look at him. His mouth had a slight quirk, and teasing humor danced in his dark eyes. She couldn't help but laugh. "Well, I think it had something to do with the champagne," she said.

The wind caught a few strands of her hair, blowing them across her face. Before she could move, Rick brought his hand up and brushed them away. His smile faded along with hers.

"Why don't you let me take you out to dinner Saturday night? Just the two of us, somewhere closer than Miami this time."

"I can't. Dolores and I have planned a party for Saturday night. A barbecue. At the resort." Abby was glad to be able to tell the truth. She liked Rick, and making up excuses had never been her style. He deserved better. "We're having dinner outside, and dancing."

Rick leaned back and looked at her thoughtfully as if he would come out and say exactly what he was thinking. But he didn't. "You'll save me a dance, then?"

A dance didn't seem like too much to ask. She found herself smiling at him. "Sure."

"Coming about," Tripp called out and the boat shifted beneath them.

Abby leaned into the turn as the sails swung across the center line. Tripp's voice must have sounded perfectly normal to everyone on the boat, but to her it seemed tight, angry. She remembered the way he'd sounded on the dock that day when Jimmy's friend had snatched the check from her hand. She glanced past Rick's shoulder and met Dolores's gaze. Dolores looked worried.

"I think I'll go below and get something to drink," Abby said. Holding on to the handrail, she carefully got to her feet. Although it must be written in *Cosmo* magazine that having two men to choose from was a feminine fantasy, having Tripp watch her with Rick, or Rick watch her with Tripp was making Abby crazy. "Would you like something?"

"I'll go with you," Rick answered.

Short of screaming and throwing herself overboard, she could think of no escape. As she and Rick made their way toward the cabin, Abby tried to read Tripp's mood. But not only was he wearing the barrier of his mirrored glasses, he didn't meet her eyes. Busy with the details of sailing, he ignored her, like he had in the months before he'd touched her.

And she watched him, like she'd been doing for longer than she'd been able to admit. The memories of his taciturn, no-nonsense attitude about the boats, about staying away from the main house, about keeping his distance from her returned. The face he showed the world seemed unshakable. Yet she had other memories. Hot, trembling, urgent memories. He was so different in the dark, in her arms, in her bed. He'd become a vital presence in her life and her heart.

Silently she promised herself and him, that as soon as Rick left Leah's Cay, they would get everything straight. It seemed like the only course of action. *The only way.* That's when she knew...for certain, the answer to her question. She couldn't accept Rick's invitation to get to know him. She'd fallen in love with Tripp, the public man and the private. Her choice would be what to do about that.

TRIPP CALLED CARLOS that evening. He'd brought the guests back safely from the sunset sail. He'd watched

Rick help Abby off the boat then walk away beside her. And he'd come close to packing his belongings and leaving.

Losing control. He'd been losing control of his life since the moment he'd turned down his partner's wife. Tripp had thought if he took the right legal steps and waited it out, that he would at least have one part of his life back. The *Wisp*. Now, even that ambition seemed thin when compared to walking away from Abby.

He couldn't sit back and wait anymore. Even though he knew Carlos's office would be closed on the weekend, he left the number of his portable phone with the answering service. He wanted to see Carlos. One way or another, with or without his boat, with or without Abby, he had to begin his life again.

He showered, dressed and headed for Miami.

ABBY WAITED for Tripp until after midnight. She'd watched him drive away in his Jeep earlier and an unexplainable feeling of vulnerability gripped her. No matter how she felt about him, she had to come to terms with the fact that Tripp could disappear from her life as suddenly as he'd appeared in it.

So she waited. Then, finally giving up hope that he would somehow come to her, she slipped between the cool sheets of her bed and turned out the light. She wasn't really surprised that he'd stayed away. After another afternoon of pretending to be strangers, of keeping secrets, she felt restless and deflated. Nothing was clear except that she loved him. And she couldn't imagine how admitting her feelings would turn out. But she intended to do just that, as soon as she had a moment alone with him.

Then there was Rick.

He deserved an answer. He'd told her the truth and deserved the same. And soon. She had to say thanks but no thanks, and let him go. Then she'd have to face Carlos.

She sighed and rearranged her pillow. Carlos would be, at the very least, disappointed. But he wasn't her father, he was her business adviser. She couldn't make love into a business deal even under the guise of good intentions. Larry had taught her that.

At least she knew Tripp wasn't after her money. The problem centered around not knowing what he did want from her. The only way to find out would be to tell him the truth about how she felt. A scary thought.

How would Tripp react when he found out she was wealthy? Could he live with the fact that she owned Leah's Cay and much more?

Unable to get comfortable, Abby pushed back the covers and got out of bed. She pushed open the French doors and stepped out on the balcony, into the night.

The ever-present breeze off the ocean had calmed to a whisper of movement along the flower-studded branches draping the railing. The ocean, beyond the shadowed expanse of lawn, was calm, the boats battened down at the dock.

Where was Tripp?

Abby caught herself holding her breath, out of fear

that if she moved too quickly, the peace would be shattered. And if that happened, the moments of happiness she'd known in the past week would disappear.

Along with Tripp.

TRIPP'S PORTABLE PHONE rang at 8:30 a.m.

"Is there a problem?" Carlos said without preamble.

"No. I need to see you, though. I'm in Miami."

He'd spent the night driving. First, from the Keys to Miami. Then he'd revisited his old life, cruising by his house in Miami Shores, which he'd sold to a young married couple. He'd even stopped by the closed offices he and his partner had shared at the boat brokerage.

He'd spent the early hours of the morning driving along the hotel strip on A1A, eaten breakfast at a diner that touted the best pancakes in the state—twenty-four hours a day—and from a bench on South Beach, had watched the sun come up. He'd saved the pilgrimage to check on his boat for this morning. After he'd talked to Carlos.

"I'm afraid I don't have good news for you."

Static buzzed like a portent through the circuit of the portable phone. "Bad news? Or just no news?"

"I had intended to tell you on Monday. I only received the papers by courier late yesterday."

More static. Carlos paused, and for a moment Tripp thought he'd lost the connection. "Are you still there?"

"Yes. Can you be at my office in forty-five minutes? I'll meet you there and we'll discuss your options."

"Yes, but tell me what's happened."

"The judge has ruled against you and Mr. Shay." Carlos's voice took on the formal, legal tone he probably used in court. "The assets in question are to be auctioned off on the twenty-first. The money used to settle debts. The remaining funds divided among the litigants."

"That's next week," Tripp said stupidly. He felt breathless and squashed, as if he'd been scuba diving and stayed down too deep, too long. The air around him seemed to be pressing inward rather than expanding. "So that's it?"

"Not quite. The boat must be sold, but there is one other option if you are interested. Meet me and we'll talk."

Tripp pressed the end button and stared out over the sand. There were only a few die-hard South Beach residents out at this hour. The sun was up and growing warmer, but the sand held the coolness of evening. He felt out of place, like a ghost hanging around his old life mumbling, "What happened? *What happened?*"

The boat must be sold. Hadn't he known that? Why had he tried to fool himself about the outcome? The last six months had been an exercise in futility. Everything he wanted stood just out of reach.

Not quite. He'd wanted Abby, and the past week had brought her to him. For better or worse. He'd lost his boat, but he'd found something with her he'd thought he could never have. Love, not merely lust. Now he knew the most important reason why he should have stayed away from her. Not because Carlos might find out. But because, unfortunately, Tripp would lose Abby, too. He had to be realistic about that. And the depth of his loss hovered on the horizon like the *Titanic*, beyond help and…taking on water.

First things first, however. Right now he had to meet Carlos, to finish the postmortem of his life. To conclude his stint as the owner of the *Wisp*.

He stood and headed for his Jeep.

"HAS ANYONE SEEN Tripp?" Abby asked the assorted people busy with different jobs in the kitchen. There were two men and one woman from the caterer, Louisa, Julia and Dolores.

Louisa wiped her hands on a towel and looked up. "No. His Jeep was gone when I came in."

Tripp had left the Cay over twenty-four hours ago and since that time, Abby's emotions had seesawed from worry, to confusion, to fear. Something was up.

Determined to act as if everything was fine, Abby turned to Dolores. She had an apron tied over her silk pantsuit, two combs arranged to pull back her dark, silver-dusted hair, and she was busy arranging appetizers on a tray. "You should be outside with the guests. What are you doing in here working?"

"I told her the same thing," Louisa added, shaking a flour-covered finger at Dolores. "You'll ruin your pretty clothes."

Dolores aimed a guilty smile at Abby. "I can't help it. I like being busy, and I love entertaining." She handed

Abby a piece of asparagus wrapped with prosciutto. "Try this, it's wonderful."

After tasting the offering, Abby had to agree, but her thoughts couldn't be swayed by food. "Well, finish that up and then come outside. I believe the band is about to start playing."

"I will, I promise," Dolores answered.

Abby moved aside to allow a man with a tray full of bar glasses go past. Then she followed him out the side entrance.

She'd just made it to the front of the house when a limo pulled up to the front steps. The driver opened the door, and Carlos Cezare exited the car before turning to help his wife.

"Good evening." Abby greeted Carlos and Virginia, then offered her hand to the couple who had accompanied them. "Welcome to Leah's Cay."

"This is lovely," Virginia said as she surveyed the grounds.

The sun had gone down but the sky remained a pinkish gold behind the silhouettes of the palm trees. The perfect vista for a "Visit Florida" postcard. Twinkling lights had been strung in the salt bushes along the drive, and portable torches gave the area a Hawaiian flavor.

"Thank you," Abby replied. "The weather is certainly cooperating. Come and meet the others." She guided them forward toward the tables set with crystal and china, where the rest of the guests were gathered. The three lawyers—Rick, Charlie and Ray—were standing together near the bar that had been set up on the veranda. Shannon and Kayla had wandered down to the dock with two young men they'd invited to the party. The honeymoon couple were seated at one of the tables, drinking champagne and listening to the music.

Lost in introductions and the duties of being the hostess, Abby had to put aside her preoccupation with Tripp's absence, although he never left her thoughts completely. She'd gone over the events of the previous day a hundred times in her mind and wished she could go back and change a few of them. The memory of Tripp's strong arms caging her at the wheel of the sailboat was the one part she didn't want to change. Unless it meant having more time with him alone. But she couldn't settle anything between them until he returned to Leah's Cay.

By the time dinner was over, Abby had begun to worry in earnest. Where was Tripp?

"Something bothering you tonight?" Rick asked as he pulled her into his arms for his promised dance. At the request of the honeymoon couple, the band was playing a slow love song. Abby's heart twisted as she looked up at him, the setting was absolutely perfect for dancing under the stars on a warm tropical night, except that she was in the arms of the wrong man.

"It's been a hectic day," she answered, sidestepping the reasons.

He studied her for a long moment before speaking. "Well, why don't you just relax now? Dinner was great, the party is a success." He angled his head in the direction of the other dancers. "Even the teenagers seem to be having a good time, and that's saying a lot."

When she didn't answer, he lowered his head next to hers. "Come on. How about five minutes of dancing and not thinking?"

His advice seemed sound. Abby relaxed in his arms and allowed his hands to guide her through the steps. She closed her eyes and did her best to empty her mind of worry, of Tripp. When the song ended, she was almost sorry. Rick stopped moving but didn't pull away. Abby opened her eyes, feeling more relaxed than she had all day, and experienced a shock like a lightning bolt out of the clear, star-filled sky. Tripp stood with Jimmy Rittner and Carlos near the railing of the veranda, but he was watching her.

She stiffened in Rick's arms and started to pull away before she realized she couldn't run over to Tripp and demand to know where he'd been. Rick looked down at her in question.

"That was less than five minutes, but I guess it'll have to do," he said as the band shifted into a faster, salsa-type song. Rick released her, but kept one hand on the small of her back as he guided her toward the tables.

Tripp's gaze never left Abby until Carlos spoke to him and forced him to pay attention. Even though he'd come back to the Cay only to pack his things and say goodbye, leaving hadn't seemed real until he'd seen Abby in Rick's arms.

Good, bad or indifferent, he hadn't confessed to loving her—not in words. And now he'd never be able to tell her. That fact twisted inside him like the shaft from a speargun.

He had no rights when it came to Abby. Never had. He'd just lost his mind for a while and accidentally handed over his heart to her. No happy ending required.

Carlos concluded his conversation with Jimmy by handing him an engraved linen business card. Jimmy pumped Carlos's hand like a man whose life has just been saved. He then followed Tripp back to the Jeep.

"I don't know how to thank you, man," Jimmy said as he arranged his crutches between the seats before pulling himself inside.

"Don't thank me yet," Tripp warned. "In a few months you may feel like you've sold your soul to the devil. Carlos is someone you better take seriously. He's all business."

"I'll do anything to keep my boat," Jimmy said earnestly.

Tripp started the engine of the Jeep, looked over his shoulder and began to back up. "Yeah, I know the feeling." He'd gotten part of what he'd wanted. Earlier in the day, Carlos had filled him in on the details of saving the *Wisp*. It would be sold to investors and, to earn his shares, Tripp would be required to captain it for charters. He would be leaving for Bermuda on his boat after the auction next week. "Be careful what you wish for."

IT TOOK FORTY MINUTES for Tripp to deliver Jimmy Rittner back to his house and return to Leah's Cay. He should have been relieved to have the *Wisp* back in the water, excited about making plans for the sail to Bermuda even if he'd only been included as a partner. But the whole time away from Leah's Cay his imagination played and replayed the sight of Abby in Rick's arms.

The party seemed to have picked up pace while he'd been gone. The music sounded faster, the laughter louder. After parking his Jeep, Tripp took the long way around the house, then stopped at the edge of the lighted area.

Carlos and his wife and another couple were dancing salsa-style, to the amazement of the teenagers and the other guests. Tripp had to hand it to the lawyer, he could loosen up and enjoy himself. And he also obviously had a long and happy relationship with his wife. They danced like a perfectly suited couple, a couple who truly knew and enjoyed each other.

Tripp's gaze shifted automatically to Abby. She looked so beautiful, her dress a bright splash of red in the torchlight. She hadn't seen him yet so he could watch her, like he'd always watched her. Seeing her in this gracious setting, standing with Rick, the man Carlos deemed as suitable, made him realize he could never tell Abby how he really felt about her. It would be a stupid and selfish thing to do. He'd already shared more with her than he'd had a right to.

Not his. She remained as unreachable as one of the sparkling constellations in the sky over their heads, as unattainable as his dream of sailing around the world on the *Wisp*. Tripp turned away when Carlos urged

Rick and Abby to try dancing salsa-style. He had enough trouble trying to find his own equilibrium, his own path away from Abby.

Abby looked up from studying the movement of Carlos and Virginia's elaborate dance steps and saw Tripp walking away. Time seemed to shift back into a series of times she'd watched him leave her. A skitter of anger flared inside her. Well, she'd had enough of his back. It was time for him to face the music, face her. She had to see his expression when she told him that she loved him. She had to know how *he* felt.

It took her fifteen minutes to find a way to leave the party unremarked. She'd ended up pulling Dolores in as a substitute dancer in her place, then she'd cut through the house, out the back door and along the path to the guest house.

She knocked on the door and waited. No answer. Instead of knocking again, she turned the knob and the door swung open.

She called his name but heard only the music from the party. The house was neat, as if he spent little time in the living area. She left the door open and walked through toward the light spilling from the bedroom. A half-packed duffel bag sat on the bed. She realized he was leaving at the same moment he walked through the bathroom door into the room. Dressed only in a towel wrapped around his waist, with his hair wet and slicked back, he'd obviously just gotten out of the shower.

"Weren't you going to say goodbye?"

14

TRIPP STARED AT ABBY for one long moment. Then he tossed the toiletry case he carried onto the bed next to his clean clothes.

"I intended to talk to you later. Alone," he said in a low serious voice, without looking at her again. He picked up the jeans off the bed and headed back into the bathroom. "I'll be out in a minute."

Abby's heart took several quick, hard beats as he closed the bathroom door. Everything from the set of his shoulders to the tone of his voice seemed ominous. He looked tired. And immovable. A terrible weak feeling blossomed inside her, inspired by the idea that he was about to walk out of her life.

Suddenly she couldn't stand next to the bed, next to the half-packed bag. She crossed her arms over her chest to keep herself together, then walked back into the living area. Through the open door, she could see the lights from the party at the main house beyond the trees. Anything she wanted, within easy reach. It all belonged to her...except Tripp.

In the bathroom, Tripp yanked on his jeans then leaned against the sink and looked in the mirror. *And what are you going to say to her?* He ran a hand over his wet hair and sighed. He could do the right thing, tell her the truth. That should make his departure more palatable, and more final. Time to do what he'd been trying to avoid.

He found her in the living room. The tension radiating from her made him want to walk up behind her and pull her into his arms. He stopped three feet away instead.

"We need to talk," he said. He watched her straighten her spine and turn toward him. Her gaze met his briefly, sadly, then lowered to his bare chest. He should have put on a shirt, he realized. That would have been the civilized thing to do. The best he could do to remedy the lapse was cross his arms and go on.

Her gaze rose to his once more. "Where are you going?"

"Away— Miami, for a while."

"Why? Did you get your boat back?"

"Sort of," he answered, feeling like a live bug twisting on a pin. The last thing he wanted to do was make Abby feel the same way. "The *Wisp*— My boat is being sold to a group of investors. I'm going along as part of the deal."

She appeared to think the statement over then step past it. "So that's it, then?" Her eyes sparkled with moisture and her hands tightened as if she was holding on for dear life. "You're out of here. See ya, wouldn't want to be ya?"

Tripp couldn't stand not touching her for one more second. He stepped forward and ran his hands up her arms to her shoulders. He wanted to hold her close, but he needed to look her in the eye when he told her the truth.

"I have to go. The deal's been made. I'm not in a position to change it."

"Would you if you could?"

"What do you mean?"

She held him prisoner with her serious eyes. "Would you stay here if you could?"

"In a perfect world, I would stay anywhere if it meant being with you," he said, and meant every word although the spark of hope that flared in her gaze made his chest hurt. "But the world isn't perfect and there are some things I can't change."

"What if you could change them? What if *I* could change them for you?"

"Abby—" He pulled her close to his chest. Her arms relaxed then slid around his bare back. With her in his arms, the words were doubly hard to say. *God, how was he going to survive letting her go and walking away?* He pushed his face into her hair, closed his eyes and tried anyway. "I have to go. I can't let you—"

"What's going on here?"

Abby jumped at the intrusive voice and Tripp's hold instinctively tightened around her. Carlos, looking furious, stood in the open doorway. And, to make matters worse, Rick was standing directly behind him.

Tripp released Abby so that she could turn, but he kept one arm along her back.

Carlos stepped through the door, his angry gaze on

Tripp. "I asked you a question. Just what do you think you are doing?"

Tripp had no suitable answer. Standing there half-dressed with Abby in his house, in his arms, anything he said would make the situation worse. Without taking his gaze from Tripp, Carlos said, "Richard? Please escort Abby back to the main house."

Rick stepped forward but Abby moved closer to Tripp. "No, I'm not going anywhere. What's going on?" She sounded shocked and confused.

Carlos turned his attention to Abby and his features softened slightly. "Abby, you know I have your best interests at heart. You must trust me on this as you've trusted me in the past." He held her gaze as if he could make her agree by sheer force of will.

Tripp watched Abby digest her lawyer's words, looking for the meaning behind them. But then she shook her head and Carlos's expression hardened again slightly. "Very well, then." He turned to Tripp.

"I want you off this estate in fifteen minutes—"

"No, wait—" Abby interrupted. "You don't understand. You have no right to blame this on Tripp."

Carlos held up a hand to stop her. "I'm afraid I understand all too well, and I'm sorry you've been hurt by this. But I trusted this man and brought him here to your house. Whatever he's done is my responsibility.

"You will allow me to remedy my mistake. Now, please, go back to the house with Richard. I will explain everything later."

"No. I have a right to be here," Abby declared.

For once in their association, Tripp agreed with Carlos. When Abby looked to him in confusion, tears sparkling in her eyes, he squeezed her close and angled her toward Rick. "Go ahead. Carlos is right." When she still resisted he added, "You know it's time for me to leave. I'll come and say goodbye before I go. I promise." He hoped she couldn't tell he was lying.

The last thing he saw was the last thing he'd wanted to see. Abby walking away, out of his life, with Rick.

TRIPP HADN'T KEPT his promise. He hadn't said goodbye. That fact repeated itself in her head over and over again like a jammed audiotape. *He's gone. He's gone. He's gone.*

Abby stared out the window of the limo at the familiar salt marshes along U.S. 1 and sighed. When she'd been certain Tripp wasn't going to show up as he'd said he would, she'd given in and cried until there weren't any tears left. Until she'd fallen into exhausted sleep. Now she was about to find out what had happened after she'd been escorted away from Tripp the night before. Carlos had sent a car and requested her presence in Miami.

She couldn't ignore the request; she had to know. Since Tripp hadn't explained, she'd have to rely on Carlos.

Dolores had insisted on accompanying her for moral support. Abby remembered another journey to Carlos's office, one she'd had to make alone. On that day two and a half years ago, her lawyer had done his duty and protected her from Larry, a man who wanted her money. She was glad that Dolores had come along today and especially grateful that she had the presence of mind not to try to talk. A sense of impending doom, mingled with the numbness of new loss, made Abby's throat so tight, she doubted she could say a word. *Tripp.*

They arrived at the building an hour and a half later. Since it was Sunday, a guard had to unlock the door in order for them to enter the sleek high-rise. After leaving the elevator, Abby paced down the tastefully decorated corridor to the carved wooden door leading into the reception area of the law office. Carlos met them there.

"How are you, dear?" Carlos said, and gave her a fatherly kiss on the cheek. He made no comment on her appearance but she could tell he was sincerely worried about her.

Abby appreciated his concern but it escalated her dread about how bad this might be. "You wanted to see me?"

He patted her shoulder. "Yes, come into my office. Mrs. Delgado, why don't you make yourself comfortable here."

A few moments later, like a recurring nightmare, Abby found herself seated at Carlos's desk as he handed her a file.

TRIPP SLAMMED THE DOOR of his Jeep and walked over to the locked chain-link fence around the dry dock. The fence didn't even slow him down. As he vaulted over the top in broad daylight, he was beyond worrying about rules or fences. He had nothing left to lose.

He walked between the smaller boats on trailers toward the water where the larger boats would be up on blocks or in slips. He found the *Wisp* second from the end.

She looked forlorn as most sailboats did when they were out of the water. But she was battened down and in good shape. With a little elbow grease she'd come alive again and bring a good price at the auction.

Frowning, Tripp decided that it was all water under the bridge now. His deal with Carlos and the investors, the final straw to keep Tripp at least a partner in the *Wisp*'s ownership had been broken the night before. The moment Carlos had seen him with his arms around Abby.

Tripp winced at the memory, but if he had it to do over again, he'd still choose to have Abby in his arms, even for a short time. Even though he'd lost his last chance.

He ran a hand along the smooth blue surface of the *Wisp*'s hull and decided he could at least console himself with the knowledge that he'd done all he could to try to keep her. Now there was only one thing left to do for the *Wisp*. Tripp could make sure whoever bought her knew how special she was. He knew just who to call.

He pulled out his portable phone and dialed directory assistance for the number of Chuck Evans, a man he'd disliked for years.

When Chuck answered, and Tripp identified himself, he almost smiled at the man's words.

"Hey, *Tripper.* I heard you were dead."

"Those rumors are greatly exaggerated," Tripp replied without missing a beat.

"So why are you calling me? You looking for a job now? You know I told you to quit that butthead Shay and come to work for me, before all the shit hit the fan."

The growing sarcasm in the Chuck's voice made Tripp wish he could tell him to shove the phone receiver somewhere private, but he held his temper. He didn't need anything from Chuck the "vampire," his former competition in the boat brokerage business.

"I'm sure you remember I didn't work for Shay. We were partners."

"Yeah, and look how that turned out," Chuck added smugly.

"I didn't call to talk over past history. I called to do you a favor," Tripp said, casting the sentence like a line with bait.

"A favor...huh? I can't wait to hear this one. Go on."

"Remember the *Wisp?*"

"Of course I remember her. What about her?"

"She's going up for sale. Next week—Friday—at auction."

"You're selling the *Wisp?*" He sounded surprised. "What did you do? Run her aground on a reef?"

"Nope, nothing like that. She's been in dry dock, needs a little loving care but otherwise she's fine."

"Why are you telling me about it?" Surprise had

shifted to caution. "There's never been any love lost between us."

Tripp wasn't in the frame of mind to go into selling mode, so he told the truth. "There hasn't been any outright bloodshed, either. What can I say? She's gonna be sold. At least I know you realize how special she is."

"And you're out of the bidding?"

"Way out. Call the Michelson Brokerage for the details."

"That's a tough break but I'll be there." Tripp could tell Chuck was grinning.

He turned for one last look at his boat, at his dreams, and felt relieved. Now if he could only make a few phone calls to get Abby back, life would be...incredible.

"BUT TRIPP NEVER WANTED money from me," Abby said after Carlos had made his case—that Tripp had seduced her to get his boat back. She felt stunned. *Not like Larry. Tripp couldn't be like Larry.* "I offered to help him and he said no."

"I've been told that's the way a good con man works. If he'd asked you to help, you'd have been suspicious." Carlos had the grace to look aggrieved in her behalf. "I didn't want to believe it either, until I saw him touching you. I trusted the man's honor, sent him there to protect you for God's sake."

Carlos stopped and in a tired gesture, ran a hand over his face. "But I was fooled. Perhaps in his situation the temptation was too great. A woman destroyed his business. He must have thought getting money from you would be justice.''

Abby looked down at Tripp's life history on the papers in front of her and sighed. His situation—hurt by a woman. He had no prior record as a con man. Yet her instincts had been right about him being more than a boat bum. He'd been a successful partner in a yacht brokerage before legal troubles between the other two partners, Robin Shay and his wife, had scuttled the business.

He'd exhausted his own resources in the fight but his lawyers couldn't stand up against the divorce court and the IRS. That's when he'd come to Carlos for help to save his boat. Both he and Carlos had cooked up this plan to protect her without her knowledge. But Tripp had lied to her. He'd seduced her and made love to her, knowing all along that she owned the resort. He must have wanted *something* from her.

"I can only think he didn't get to the point of asking for money because I intervened," Carlos said.

Abby had to agree that much was true. She remembered Larry's careful plans, his smiling harmlessness—all of which had fallen apart when Carlos intervened with the truth.

But there had been nothing careful or harmless about Tripp. And he'd always seemed to be backing away. She remembered his words in the pool, in the bar, about them making a mistake. Was his reluctance a lie also? A ruse?

Abby rubbed her forehead with her palm, unable to

think about her and Tripp anymore. He'd left without saying goodbye; how much more did she need to know? "What about his boat? Did you get it back for him?"

Carlos stiffened in his seat and his mouth shifted into a straight unhappy line. "I had made arrangements with a group of investors to buy his boat back at auction on Friday. He would have been made a lesser partner and be allowed to captain the boat for high-end charters out of Bermuda." When Abby didn't comment, Carlos shrugged. "It was the best I could do in the situation. But now the deal is dead. He has broken his word to me and I will not help him in any way."

Abby felt like they'd all been hurt in one way or another. But ultimately, the man sitting across from her had started the whole thing.

"You know? If you'd told me the truth about him in the first place, everything would have been different."

Carlos had the class to nod sadly. "I know."

FEELING like a sleepwalker, Abby made it downstairs to the car before she started crying again.

Dolores put a comforting arm around her shoulders then dug in her bag for a tissue to offer to Abby.

Abby leaned her head back and sighed. "What a big mess."

"What happened?"

"Oh, the usual," she answered, blinking back tears. "Another man with a crush on my money."

"You mean Tripp? Are you sure? I saw him look at

you with his heart in his eyes. It's hard to believe it was an act."

She dabbed at her eyes with the tissue. "Carlos is sure." He'd presented her with the cold hard facts.

"What do you think?"

Abby remembered Tripp, climbing through her window in a storm, holding her after making love to her, the expression on his face as he'd watched her dance with Rick. Night heat. The memory of it softened and warmed the quaking pain inside her. She couldn't equate those actions to a man after her money. She didn't want to. Feelings were safer than thoughts.

"Thinking hurts," she said truthfully, then looked her friend in the eye. "He lied to me about why he was at Leah's Cay, then he left without explaining or saying goodbye. I don't know the reasons. I guess I'll never know. But the whole thing looks pretty damning. Like I said, a big mess."

"Do you love him?"

Abby should have been ready for the question, but she wasn't. Dolores had tried to ask her before and she'd been afraid to consider the answer. Now the answer didn't matter.

"Yes, for all the good it does me."

"Now wait a minute," Dolores said in her best mothering voice. "You are acting like you have no say in this matter."

"What do you mean?"

"If you love him, then do something about it."

"Like what?"

"Tomas used to say that one of the best things about having money...was having influence. People would go out of their way to get things done when the price was right."

"What does that have to do with me loving Tripp? Are you saying I should buy his love?"

"No, dear." Dolores smiled and squeezed her arm. "But what if Carlos is wrong? Can you live with not knowing? You are a very rich woman. If you want to speak to Tripp again or find out what has happened to him, all you have to do is ask the right people and offer the right price. You don't need Carlos."

RICK WAS SEATED on the veranda when the limo stopped at the front of the house. He was dressed for travel in a shirt and tie, his jacket hung over the back of an empty chair. He rose from his seat when Abby stepped out of the car.

"How are you?" he asked, and kissed her lightly on the cheek.

Abby gazed up into the sincere look of distress on his face and wished she'd discovered him before she'd fallen so hopelessly in love with Tripp. "I'm okay," she lied.

"You two sit down. I'll have Louisa bring out some ice tea," Dolores said as she shooed Abby forward into the chair Rick pulled out for her.

"Thanks, Dee," Abby managed. She sat down in the chair and looked out toward the ocean. Leah's Cay was as beautiful as it had always been but for Abby, it held little peace today. Tripp was gone and she wondered if she'd ever be able to forget his presence here and in her heart.

The other guests were suspiciously absent. Several of them were leaving today, including Rick, and were probably packing.

"I feel like I owe you an apology," Abby said, keeping her eyes on the tropical blue water in the distance. If she looked at him, she'd probably start to cry again.

"No, you don't," he answered. "You don't owe anyone anything."

She looked at him. "But I wasn't completely honest with you. I should have told you about Tripp and me. I never meant—"

He raised a hand to stop her. "I understand about bad timing. And we can't always help who we fall in love with."

A few moments of silence followed that statement. Abby wondered if everyone had seen all along what was happening between her and Tripp. Then the door swung open and Louisa appeared with a tray of glasses and a pitcher. After Abby thanked her, they were left alone again.

Rick picked up the pitcher and poured. "So I guess you're not going to take me up on my proposal."

As usual, he had taken her off guard. When she met his gaze, he smiled but she sensed regret. "I wish I could, but you deserve someone who loves you the first time she sets eyes on you. The kind of love that has nothing to do with old family names, or business deals, or money."

He shrugged as if that would never happen. "What *are* you going to do?"

"I don't know." Abby sighed. "I'd like to find some closure on the whole thing but that would involve finding Tripp. Carlos has severed all ties and threatened him because he thinks he's after my money." She frowned at the thought but continued. "As much as it hurts me to say it, I suppose he was."

Rick appeared to consider that statement for a moment. "I don't know. Tripp didn't seem like the type. He was too rough around the edges. Con men are usually slicker." He smiled. "More like me."

A small smile rose inside Abby. "What do you think I should do?"

Rick sat back and took a drink of tea before answering. "Well, when this happened to me and I wasn't sure whether Celie wanted me or my money, I gave her what she wanted, which was a big house out on the West Coast. I secretly hoped she'd turn it down and stay on the East Coast with me, because she loved me." With a clunk he set the tea glass back on the table. "That was three years ago. She really loved that house."

Abby wasn't sure what to say, until Rick smiled and shrugged again. "An expensive test," she finally commented.

"I suppose. But it was cheaper and less painful than making her my wife for all the wrong reasons." He paused and gazed at the ocean before continuing. "And you know what? I cared about her enough to give her what she really wanted. I could afford it, it made her happy and it got her out of my life."

Tripp was already out of her life, but not out of her heart. Abby realized she had the power to give him what he wanted, too. Of course. The *Wisp*. "Tripp needed money to get his sailboat back," she said, then looked at Rick.

"Why don't you give it to him and see what he does?"

15

TRIPP HAD WANTED TO stay away, but he found he couldn't. Watching the *Wisp* be sold would be like attending his own funeral—the funeral of his dreams anyway. Yet, he had to be there.

He had to search for a parking space in the marina lot that was already filled with Mercedes, Jaguars and Cadillacs. He finally squeezed his Jeep into a grassy space between two boats. What could they do? Tow him?

Attending this sale would be his final act as a Florida resident. On Monday, he'd be flying to the Bahamas, to work for a boat broker there, to make a new start. He couldn't stay in Miami—it was too close to the Keys, too close to Leah's Cay.

And he knew he wouldn't be able to stay away forever. He'd already driven down to the Pelican Bar twice and it wasn't quite a week since he'd left Abby. Left her without explaining, without telling her that he loved her, without saying how damned sorry he was about everything. If he stayed, it would only be a matter of time before he drove up to the house. Then both Abby and Carlos would probably have him arrested as a stalker.

He needed to put a lot of ocean between himself and Abby. Because being on land hadn't helped him forget her, nor did it make him feel better about the way he'd left things between them. If the Bahamas didn't suffice then he'd try the West Coast.

He deserved to lose both his boat and Abby. He'd done everything wrong. Now he had to say his last goodbye to the *Wisp*. He walked between two limos parked close to the door of the marina offices and nodded to the drivers, standing together talking. One of them looked familiar but it couldn't be Carlos's driver. Unless Carlos had decided to buy the *Wisp* anyway, because it was a good investment.

Tripp opened the door and stepped into the air-conditioned presentation room. Nearly every chair that had been set up for the auction was filled, and the sale was underway. At least fifty people looking for bargains with checkbooks to back up their bids were listening to the description of the next item.

Tripp made his way around the side of the room but remained standing near the wall as the bidding began for one of the smaller boats listed. He spied Chuck, the man he'd called a few days before about the *Wisp* and nodded to him.

Then he saw Abby.

His heart pounded with several hard kicks. He thought he had to be hallucinating. *What the hell was she doing here?* But he blinked and there she remained, seated off to one side on the front row. She hadn't spotted him yet, she was speaking to the man sitting next to

her. Tripp realized the man was Rick, just before Abby
looked up and met his gaze across the crowded room.

She didn't smile or seem surprised to see him.

He felt her appraisal like a punch to the sternum.
Even dressed in a soft businesslike jacket and skirt, she
set off every neuron under his skin. The memories of
holding her, touching her, loving her, couldn't be
blocked by the camouflage of her conservative clothes.
He knew what she looked like naked. He could hardly
breathe. He didn't want to move, unless it was across
the room to her. He traced her features with the greed
of a man who'd been lost in dreams too long and
needed reality.

Why had she come here?

"Now we have lot number 23," the auctioneer announced. "The *Wisp*, a forty-foot sou'wester yawl."

Tripp listened halfheartedly to the bids being made.
He didn't realize Abby held a paddle with a number on
it, until she raised it.

"That's one hundred twenty-five thousand from
number 44. Do I hear one-fifty?"

Tripp's arch nemesis, Chuck, offered one fifty.

When the gavel came down the last time, selling the
Wisp for two hundred thousand, the auctioneer smiled.
"Sold to the lovely lady in the first row."

By the time Tripp made it around the room, Abby
was already signing the check.

Abby's hand was shaking as she signed her name.
Not because she'd just spent two-hundred-thousand

dollars on a boat, but because she was about to get what she wanted, to talk to Tripp one last time.

"What the hell are you doing?" he asked as she accepted the completed papers from the auction cashier.

The sound of his voice set off a series of new tremors through to her knees but she turned to face him. She had to brazen it out. "I just bought a boat," she said, making the statement sound offhand. But then she made the mistake of looking into his sky blue eyes. The frantic beat of her heart nearly cut off her breath.

"My boat," he said.

"Yes," she managed to say. "Would you like to show it to me?"

Before he could answer or move, a man pushed up next to them. Abby realized he'd been the other serious bidder on the *Wisp*. With a tight smile he handed her his card. "If you change your mind, call me." The look he gave Tripp might have worried her, if Tripp had paid any attention to him whatsoever. His eyes remained on her and as the desk became crowded with the next buyers, he took her arm and led her toward the door.

Rick stepped in front of them, forcing them to stop. "I'll wait in the car," he said to Abby in a voice that sounded like a warning for Tripp. She almost smiled but she didn't want to spoil the charade they'd planned together. Instead, she patted his arm.

"I'll be there in a few minutes," she answered.

Once outside, Tripp seemed to lose all interest in talking. Holding her arm in a firm grip, he directed her down the lines of boats until he reached the one he'd been looking for. Abby read the name on the stern. The *Wisp.*

Under the shadow of his boat—her boat for the moment—Tripp released her arm and turned to face her. The marina area was fairly deserted since most of the people were inside at the auction.

"What the hell do you think you're doing?" His voice came out like a growl.

Abby reined in her nervousness, determined to finish what she'd started. "I know how much this boat means to you. So I bought it."

Tripp ran a hand over his neck and looked away. "I can't let you do this. You don't need another sailboat."

"I've already done it," Abby said, pausing to brush an imaginary piece of lint from her sleeve. If she didn't do something with her hands, she would reach for him. "You don't have to worry, I can afford it."

Looking bewildered, Tripp shook his head then sighed. "I'm sorry I lied to you."

Abby shrugged. "I lied to you, too. I guess we're even."

A lengthy silence stood between them as they stared at each other. Then a horn beeped and Abby heard Rick call her name. She pushed the ownership papers into his hand. "These are for you, signed and sealed."

Tripp couldn't have looked more surprised if she'd slapped him. "What are you talking about?"

"The boat. She's yours. I hope you find what you've been looking for." She made it two steps past him before he caught her arm. As he spun her around she saw Rick headed in their direction.

"I can't take this," Tripp said. He gripped her shoulders and pulled her until they were nearly nose to nose. "What are you trying to do?"

Abby's entire body reacted to his touch and to the closeness of the hard mouth that haunted her dreams. Her heart desperately wished he would kiss her and tell her he loved her not the damned boat, but her logic required her to finish what she'd started. She was so nervous, she had to wet her lips to speak.

"I bought it because I want you to have it."

"Damn it. I don't want it."

Abby looked into his intense blue gaze and tried her best to smile although she could feel her bottom lip tremble with the effort. "Yes, you do," she whispered.

"Abby?" Rick's voice sounded close by. The cavalry.

Abby pushed back out of Tripp's grasp and glanced in Rick's direction.

"Goodbye," she said, and stepped past Tripp.

IT TOOK ABBY nearly three hours to get back to Leah's Cay. She'd had the driver deliver Rick to the airport in Miami for his delayed return home. Saying goodbye to him had been the one bright spot of the afternoon since he'd made her laugh by thanking her for such an *interesting* vacation. By the time he kissed her briefly and wished her well, she'd had tears in her eyes.

Exhausted and heartsick, she'd returned home and

allowed Dolores and Louisa to fuss over her until she pleaded for a little solitude.

The sun had set before she changed into a pair of shorts and escaped outside. The sky, still bright in the west had already shifted to a deep blue over the ocean. The first stars of the evening twinkled on the horizon. Abby walked along the dock then down the pathway to the pool. Nothing had changed, the view remained spectacular, the pool inviting. But everything looked different to her, felt different. Memories of Tripp had altered the vision of her life, and the future looked colorless without him.

She was beginning to realize that her home would never be the same, because her heart had left Leah's Cay along with Tripp.

She wondered what he was doing. Was he on his boat with the wind in his face? Happy to be back where he belonged? She hoped so. Rick had been right about one thing. It had made her feel better to give Tripp what he wanted, even though she'd hoped he'd want her more.

At the edge of the pool, Abby kicked off her sandals, sat down and dangled her feet in the water near the stairs at the shallow end. She drew in a deep breath. It was such a beautiful evening. The memory of the night she and Tripp had made love in the pool sent a shiver of pleasure through her. She didn't regret touching him, knowing him. She didn't even regret falling in love, except that now she had to come to terms with living without him.

She'd given him the boat and he hadn't refused it. He

had what he wanted. He would be off sailing around the world, chasing his dream, but she still had a resort to run. And if she got tired of that, she could do some traveling herself.

There would be no more lies, however. She'd constructed her own trap by lying to everyone about her money, by trying to protect herself. Then in the middle of it, she'd fallen in love with Tripp and had had no way out.

She slowly kicked her feet in the water, her gaze following the ripples spreading across the surface of the pool. When they reached the far side, she glanced upward and saw Tripp standing at the edge watching her.

Unable to move, Abby felt suspended in time. He stared at her for what seemed like an eternity before he made his way toward her. By the time he reached her, she had stumbled to her feet.

Tripp didn't know what to say. He knew what he had to do, but words deserted him. So without speaking, he simply drew her into his arms and kissed her until she kissed him back, until he knew she wanted to be kissed—by him. He tasted her lips, her tongue, her heat. When he got to the point where he didn't want to stop at her mouth, he pulled away.

"I've missed you," he breathed into her hair.

She didn't speak, but her fingers tightened in the material of his shirt.

Well, he figured he was on a roll so he might as well go for it. "I love you," he confessed.

Abby went completely still. Then slowly, reluctantly,

she leaned back out of his embrace to look into his eyes. She blinked at the moisture gathering in hers. "What?" she asked, her voice barely a whisper.

"I love you," he repeated in a stronger tone. It felt good to say it, to finally tell her. "I'm sorry I didn't tell you before. Everything was so screwed up with Carlos and the boat and...us. But I want you to know now." He brought one hand up to cradle her cheek, to hold her steady. "I love you. I never should have touched you, but I couldn't stay away."

She swallowed, and two trails of wetness streaked down her skin, yet she couldn't seem to speak.

"It's okay. I don't expect anything from you. I just couldn't leave again without saying goodbye and without giving you this." He reached into his top pocket and took out a check from Chuck the boat vampire. A check for two hundred thousand dollars. He took Abby's hand and pushed the paper into it.

"It's for the *Wisp*. She's gone."

Abby stared down at the check then looked back at him. "But I thought—"

He held up a hand to stop her. "I thought it was what I wanted, too. But that was before I met you." He couldn't resist brushing her cheek with his fingers again. He wanted her so much, it hurt. "I wish we could start all over again, meet for the first time. Maybe then I could get things right."

"Why can't we?"

"Because I'm who I am, and you're who you are. No

one would believe I wasn't after your money. Carlos would probably—"

"I don't care what Carlos thinks," Abby interrupted, seeming to grow stronger by the second. "Or anyone else for that matter. If you...love me..."

"I do."

She smiled shyly, looking very brave. "Then I'm the only one who has to believe."

He kissed her again, just to feel her in his arms after being away so long. When he came up for air once more, her tears had disappeared. "Do you think you could love a man with few assets but good prospects, who can't keep his hands off you?"

He'd tried to make the question sound light, teasingly unimportant, but he'd never been more serious in his life.

The answer shone in the brilliance of a smile that nearly took his breath away. "I already do."

Epilogue

THE DECK OF THE BOAT they'd named *Blue Heaven*, rocked gently under him as Abby dove over the side. Tripp leaned back into the shade of the mast and watched the graceful arc of her body cut through the crystal-clear water scattering the colorful fish under the boat. She was naked.

He'd join her soon, but first he wanted to watch her, to enjoy the pure pleasure of knowing that when he reached for her, she would settle into his arms, smiling.

He'd thought to visit Saint Thomas but they hadn't made it that far yet. They'd been in this inlet a week without seeing another human. It suited Tripp just fine. *Having no plan and sticking to it*. That's what a honeymoon was for.

The serious face of Carlos Cezare rose in his memory and he smiled. The lawyer's blessing had come along with a blizzard of paperwork and several severe lectures. Tripp didn't care. He had what he wanted—Abby. He also had a business to run when he returned. He and Jimmy Rittner were going to be a force to be reckoned with in the Keys charter-boat business.

About fifteen feet out, Abby came up for air, pushed

Night Heat

her wet hair back and grinned at him. "I'll race you to the island," she taunted.

When Tripp rose to his feet, she set off with a strong stroke toward the deserted white beach. Keeping an eye on her progress, Tripp unhurriedly levered off his deck shoes and dropped his cutoffs. She'd never make it to the beach. He'd catch her before that. And he'd make love to her in water so blue, it was difficult to tell where ocean ended and heaven began.

His heaven had already begun. His job was to look out for her, to love her. He could do that. No sweat.

THE MEN OF BACHELOR CREEK

Alaska. A place where men could be men—and women were scarce!

To Tanner, Joe and Hawk, Alaska was the final frontier. They'd gone to the ends of the earth to flee the one thing they all feared—MATRIMONY. Little did they know that three intrepid heroines would brave the wilds to "save" them from their lonely bachelor existences.

Enjoy

#662 CAUGHT UNDER THE MISTLETOE!
December 1997

#670 DODGING CUPID'S ARROW!
February 1998

#678 STRUCK BY SPRING FEVER!
April 1998

by Kate Hoffmann

Available wherever Harlequin books are sold.

HARLEQUIN®
Temptation

DEBBIE MACOMBER

invites you to the

HEART OF TEXAS

Join Debbie Macomber as she brings you the lives and loves of the folks in the ranching community of Promise, Texas.

If you loved Midnight Sons—don't miss Heart of Texas! A brand-new six-book series from Debbie Macomber.

Available in February 1998 at your favorite retail store.

Heart of Texas by Debbie Macomber

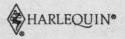

HARLEQUIN®

HPHRT1

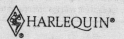

Free Gift Offer

With a Free Gift proof-of-purchase
from any Harlequin® book, you can receive
a beautiful cubic zirconia pendant.

This stunning marquise-shaped stone is a genuine cubic
zirconia—accented by an 18" gold tone necklace.
(Approximate retail value $19.95)

Send for yours today...
compliments of ◈HARLEQUIN®

To receive your free gift, a cubic zirconia pendant, send us one original proof-of-purchase, photocopies not accepted, from the back of any Harlequin Romance®, Harlequin Presents®, Harlequin Temptation®, Harlequin Superromance®, Harlequin Love & Laughter®, Harlequin Intrigue®, Harlequin American Romance®, or Harlequin Historicals® title available at your favorite retail outlet, together with the Free Gift Certificate, plus a check or money order for $1.65 U.S./$2.15 CAN. (do not send cash) to cover postage and handling, payable to Harlequin Free Gift Offer. We will send you the specified gift. Allow 6 to 8 weeks for delivery. Offer good until March 31, 1998, or while quantities last. Offer valid in the U.S. and Canada only.

Free Gift Certificate

Name: _____

Address: _____

City: _____ State/Province: _____ Zip/Postal Code: _____

Mail this certificate, one proof-of-purchase and a check or money order for postage and handling to: HARLEQUIN FREE GIFT OFFER 1998. In the U.S.: 3010 Walden Avenue, P.O. Box 9071, Buffalo NY 14269-9057. In Canada: P.O. Box 604, Fort Erie, Ontario L2Z 5X3.

FREE GIFT OFFER   084-KEZ

ONE PROOF-OF-PURCHASE
To collect your fabulous FREE GIFT, a cubic zirconia pendant, you must include this original proof-of-purchase for each gift with the properly completed Free Gift Certificate.

084-KEZR2